Antonia Nicole Savu

Lili Grace

The Spheres of Eris

2023 @ LUX MUNDI

CIP description of the National Library of Romania

SAVU, ANTONIA NICOLE

Lili Grace: The Spheres of Eris / Antonia Nicole Savu - Bucureşti: Lux Mundi, 2023

Index

ISBN 978-606-95666-8-8

821.135.1

Book design & cover: Oana Savu

editura@luxmundi.ro

For my mother, father, and brother.

I love you even when I'm not saying it.

I'll love you forever and always.

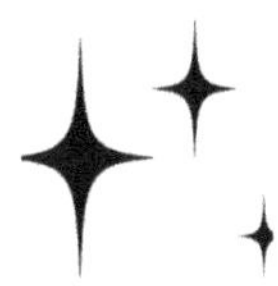

FOREWORD

This is the second foreword I have written, and I want to start by saying what a foreword means to me.

For me, a foreword is like a piece of backstory, like a journal entry, where I can tell you the story's journey from where it has begun. This is where I can tell you what this story means to me. It is where I can tell you my thought process when writing this book. I hope one day I'll be interviewed and asked more about my book and the things my characters did, and why they did that. Then, I could write about my thought process for this book and the future ones in the series.

Now, I'll share the backstory of it.

This idea came into my mind in the summer of 2022, when I was on vacation in Greece. I don't remember how the idea came to me; I remember it being in my brain. I didn't write it in my notebook; I just had it in my brain for the entire vacation.

The only thing I know for sure is that when I came up

with the idea, I searched for a book about witches. The problem was that I searched for a book with a specific type of witch but didn't find one. Who knows? Maybe there is a book with the same type of witches Lili is, and I haven't had the luck to find it. But even if there is a book with this type of a witch and I did not find it, I consider *I had the luck not to find a book like this.*

While writing this book, I wrote some paragraphs the size of the texts that teachers put me to do for school. As a result, the sections in the book took only a few minutes to write, while the texts for school sometimes took hours (I am talking about the argumentative texts).

I started writing this book on Monday, July 11, 2022, at 02:52 PM and finished writing it on January 24, 2023, at 12:55:57 PM.

The first draft of the book was done the day before my birthday, which for me means a lot, knowing that the first draft was finished just before I turned fourteen.

I always saw this as being the "prolog" of the series.

The introduction to Lili's world. If I wanted it to be a single edition, well, it would be thick as heck. My head hurts just thinking about how long it would've been.

However, with the help of my family, I realized that it was a bit too long for the first book in the series.

I wrote this book in the summer before seventh grade, and I hope it will be published while I am in seventh grade. I have in mind a date for when I want it to be published, but I don't know if it will happen. (It didn't happen, but that's OK.)

The title was probably the hardest thing to think about. I knew the series' name from the start; I wanted it to be the main character's name: Lili Grace. But the title of the book? No! I had two ideas: one better fitting for the second book and one I felt I had given too much away. In the end, I managed to choose one.

A lot of the characters took something from me. Most of them took a part of my personality. Lili, for example, took a significant part of my personality. She took the book lover, animal lover, nature lover, Greek mythology lover, magic lover (and the list is so much longer) part of me.

Some characters took a part of the personality of my friends and family, while most of my characters have the nature that I created just for them.

For me, the story of Lili's life is something that I never expected I'll ever write in my life. Since I was little, I have loved magic, witches, and all that stuff. So when the story idea came to my mind, I realized I could finally give my one take on magic and make it memorable.

At the end of the book, I realized that everything I wrote came from my imagination and mind. And, for some reason, that realization hit me harder than I thought.

I'll end this foreword like the other one I wrote, with a note to remind you that I'm doing this for myself.

English isn't my first language, but it's my go-to language when I want to write something. For the last year and a half, I started thinking more in English than Romanian, which meant that all my ideas came to my mind in English, and it was tough for me to translate them into Romanian and then put them on paper. I also remember that at one point, I was reading one of the Percy Jackson and the Olympians books, and the book was in Romanian. Still, as I was reading, I realized that my brain saw the words and translated them into English so that I saw the words in Romanian, but I heard them in my head in English.

I'm telling you those things, so you will understand that the book isn't perfect. Nothing I'll ever write would be perfect. I'm still young and learning the world's ways, but one thing is for sure; this is what I want. I'm not perfect; my books won't be perfect. People might love my books, or they might hate them. It's their opinion.

I'll celebrate when my first book is sold. When my tenth book is sold, I'll celebrate. I'll celebrate when my hundred

books are sold. When my thousand books would be sold...
well, I'll see.

After all, one thing's for sure: you will hear about me
again.

Let's jump straight into the story with no other words to
say.

Disclaimer

The witches in this book and any future book are my own take on witches. Any cultural similarity is a pure coincidence. And please DO NOT USE any of the spells that might appear in this or any other book. I created them and do not want anything to happen to anyone because of them.

Thank you!

Three years before

"Get her!" he screamed at his wife.

They ran to the back door and followed the young witch. She was fast, but not as fast as she should be. One wrong step and she fell on the ground. She tried to get up, but the hunters were quicker. They raised her by the arms so her legs couldn't touch the ground.

"It seems we have a witch on our hands, Sable," he said. The witch was stared down by his red eyes. She tried to kick them, to bite them, to escape, but the man was strong, and the woman put a knife to her throat.

The young witch tried thinking about how else she could escape. Her wand was in her boot; she could not get it. She thought about what she could do. A spell her mother tried teaching her a long time ago. The memory of that magic was foggy, but she felt she could do it.

She concentrated on what she could remember from it. All of a sudden, red fume started surrounding her. That wasn't what it was supposed to do. The hunters froze in their places, their skin turning stone cold. The grass turned brown. When the fume disappeared, the witch didn't think twice about running away.

Later, she would find out that she used one of the forbidden spells no witch should use.

Two years and two months before

It's been ten months since she escaped The Hunters. Ten months of stumbling on streets and fields and woods. She lived off of food people let out next to the garbage. Her dress, which was once white and long, was now torn apart and brown. Her hair was as tangled as a bird's nest. She tried braiding it so it wouldn't get even more tangled.

When she walked into a town, all the eyes were on her.

In time, she heard that a family was away from town for a week. She took the opportunity and went to their house. She had enough time to bathe and detangle her hair, but the family came before her hair could dry.

She could've gone to her cousin's village, but she did not know where it was, nor what its name was, it was a small village. She could've gone back to her town, but she didn't know the name of it to ask for directions. She made her guide put a spell on her so she would not remember. It was a dumb reckless move from her one late night after wandering the streets for hours.

When the snow started to settle, she was walking in some woods. From where she was, she could hear a river. Maybe she could drink its water? As she got closer, she saw a cabin on a hill in the middle of a meadow. It seemed old but a good enough place to spend a few nights. She could see the chimney, which probably meant it had a fireplace, which also meant she could warm herself up.

Chapter 1

Demons shouldn't be able to have children, but here I am, telling you about my life.

My name is Lili Grace, and I am... *something*. The creature I am doesn't have a name, given that I am the only one of my kind. I don't even know what I am.

My father is a demon, and my mother's a witch. I don't know how it happened; it shouldn't have happened. My mother never told me. Demons don't have a physical form. They can take one by possessing someone's body. My father didn't do that. He never did that. But, somehow, I am here.

The sun is up, shining, with no clouds blocking its way. I felt the grass tingle my knees. The air blew powerfully. It was pretty hot for a late afternoon spring day, but I enjoyed my time in the meadow. I took some tomatoes and lettuce from my vegetable patches.

After spending the last few years in the meadow, I learned something about it. The meadow contains herbs, mushrooms, rocks, fruit trees, vegetables, crystals, and more. I also learned that the meadow has its own rules. If I don't follow its rules, it will kick me out. It has a mind of its own.

I gently put the hair behind my ear and all the vegetables in my braided basket.

I walked through the open door of my log cabin. When I found the meadow, the cabin was already there. The only thing I had to do was put some protection spells on it and on the meadow.

The cabin wasn't big, but it was big enough for me. It was just a room and a bathroom, nothing more. Most of the furniture I needed was already in it. I only had to make a few chairs and fix the legs of the table.

The other thing that I found in the cabin - that means a lot to me - is my sweet cat, Nyx. He was just a little kitten. He sat on the corner of the bed, shaking from the cold. I remember taking him in my arms, trying to warm him up. Then, I started a fire in the fireplace and sat with the kitten on my lap, petting him. His black fur reminded me of the goddess Nyx, and his name remained that.

After I placed the basket on the table, I went to wash my hands, almost tripping over the cat.

I picked him up. "Nyx, what are you doing on the floor?" he started to purr in my hands as I placed him in his bed.

I changed from my dirty clothes to a white puffy-sleeved shirt that I made from some of the fabrics I found under the bed. Over the shirt, I put on a sleeveless button-up dress.

As I took the basket from the table, I couldn't help but notice that Nyx was gone. I usually leave the door open for him so he can get out of the house. But I didn't bother looking for him because he always returned in about an hour.

An hour passed. And another one. And then another one.

Only then, I started to worry. Nyx has never disappeared for this long. Ultimately, I began looking for him in the cabin, only to find nothing.

When the fourth hour passed, I decided to search for him outside. I put my wand in my left boot and took the black cloak from the hanger.

I took a look at the entire meadow. In the dim light of the moon, the meadow looked like a place from one of the fairy tales my mother used to tell me when I was little.

The cabin was on one of the hill. The taller hill I used for stargazing. The crops were in the back of the cabin, while the fruit trees were on the opposite part of the meadow. A river flew around the meadow, like a snake around its prey.

My eyes drifted to the tall trees of the forest. Looking at it made me feel like Nyx was somewhere in it. It wouldn't be a first for him. Most of the time, he doesn't like being outside the magical barrier I created.

I took the wand from my boot and made a light spell. On top of it, a ball of light appeared. This was the first spell I learned. I can still remember how proud my mother was.

She didn't channel her magic through a wand. She used her hands like most witches do. When it came to me, my mother said that it would be best to use a wand; at least, until I was old enough.

My mother always told me that things would slowly get better. If things slowly getting better meant her dying when I was eleven, things are "clearly better". It took me six months to find the meadow and Nyx. Since that day, Nyx has been my only family, and I won't allow him to get hurt.

As I stepped out of the meadow, I began to feel afraid. I was stepping out of the magic circle for the first time in years.

I adventure more and more into the woods. But, unfortunately, the further I got, the colder the air got.

Every tree seemed to be frozen. Not a single bird sang the song of the night. The everlasting sound of the river stopped. The temperature dropped so hard that the leaves froze.

I looked at the ground, seeing the black cat with a mouse in his mouth. Happily, the mouse was still alive.

"Nyx!" I raised my voice at him. "Leave the poor mouse alone!"

After the cat left the mouse on the ground, I took him in my hands and watched the little mouse make its way out of our area.

"You left the meadow only to catch a little mouse?" I said, expecting more from him. But he didn't even look at me. Instead, he jumped out of my hands and started hissing at the air.

It isn't normal for the temperature to drop this much in only a few minutes. This only happens when she is around.

I realized that Nyx wasn't hissing at the air; he was hissing at what was hiding in the air. Suddenly, something started to materialize, a human-shaped demon.

"Lili. Long time no see!", said the demoness.

"What do you want, Eris?" I yelled at her.

"You know very well what I want." She snarled while moving around me. "I want your soul and power. I thought you understood this during our last encounter. Didn't you?"

I wanted to kill her on the spot like I had wanted to do many times before, but I knew that my powers weren't strong enough. "You know you can't get my power nor my soul. I got protection necklaces and spells! You can't even get into my meadow!"

"We'll see about that later, my dear," she said so that I could practically hear the smirk in her voice. "Everyone wants something. I only have to know what you want."

"I don't want anything from you!"

"Maybe love... safety?"

I don't know how she knew what I wanted. All I knew was that Eris would never give me what I wanted, no matter what I would do for her. She's just a power-hungry demon.

"Maybe... your mother."

I couldn't move. I barely managed to say something. "Don't you dare bring my mother into this, you demon!" My voice was so high that I even scared myself from how I shouted.

"Look at you!" she said, pointing at me with her transparent finger. "A thirteen-year-old ordering ME! A four-thousand-year-old demoness! Pathetic! I thought you knew that there was no way of stopping me. I'm invincible. Unstoppable! I will always get what I want. No matter the price."

I held my wand in my right hand and pointed it to Eris, and put a destruction spell on her. As I expected, it didn't work, but it might make her confused enough for me to buy some time, so I could make myself disappear.

"Where do you think you're going, dear?"

"To safety," I responded.

"There's no safe place for you in this world!"

"You really are obsessed with me! You've been trying to get rid of me since I was a baby! You can't get enough of me! And here's my question: Why?"

"You know why. You're the greatest witch that will ever exist in our world, Lili. You're the only one who can destroy me! So I'll destroy you before you can destroy me!" said the demoness with a big smirk on her transparent face before attacking me.

She started slashing my skin with her sharp fume nails. She shouldn't be able to cut me, but she had tricks that no one would think about.

I tried protecting myself with spells, but the more she cut my skin open, the weaker my spells became.

She scratched my right cheek with her nails and then opened the corner of my lip. The metallic taste of blood started to enter my mouth slowly.

Eris gave one final cut. I fell on my knees, holding my stomach. When I took my hand off it, my hand was full of blood. The scarlet color of blood shone in the moonlight.

The demoness left me in the wood, thinking I'll probably die sooner or later.

I managed to get on my feet and stumble through the woods. I walked, not knowing what direction to take. My sight became blurrier with every step I took. I didn't want to admit it. My brain couldn't process the fact that I might be dying. I had just so little time until I would turn fourteen. This couldn't be the end of my story.

There was a part of me that wanted to die. I don't like to admit that. That part was the part that would've done anything to see my mother again.

I stopped for a moment. I heard the sound of leaves moving. The figure of a boy started emerging from the bushes in front of me.

I tried asking for help, but I didn't have any power to speak. Finally, my legs went numb, and I fell onto the cold ground.

The boy rushed to my side. He kneeled next to my body.

His eyes were the brightest blue I have ever seen. "Did you know your eyes look like sapphire?" I asked him, reaching with my hand for his cheek.

Chapter 2

Most of my dreams are visions.

When I was eight, I dreamed that my cousin and I were riding horses, and when we stopped by his mother's house, I'd fall off the horse and break my leg.

From the moment that happened in reality, my mother never let me on a horse.

Now I appeared to be walking through a hallway as grand and big as one in a castle. It didn't seem like the guards were noticing me.

I stopped in front of some large open doors. Inside the room, I saw people dressed elegantly; no place for a witch like me.

But my dream was cut short, before it could become more complex.

My eyes opened like I woke up from a nightmare. My heart was rushing faster than at any other time. The smell in the air wasn't what I was used to waking up to.

I looked at the room. A closet by the door. A couch under the window. A desk in front of the bed, under another window. A bookshelf by the bed I was in.

I thought about how I ended up here. All I could remember were the sapphire eyes I saw before passing out.

I tried getting up from the bed to look out the window, but hissed in pain.

If it wasn't for the memory of Eris cutting my flesh open, I wouldn't have thought to look at my body.

My hands were bandaged all the way up from my wrists to my shoulders. My legs only had minor scratches. I looked at the place where Eris gave her last cut and saw that the bandages were covered in a dark maroon-red shade.

The white shirt and beige dress didn't survive either and were stained with blood.

The door on the left wall opened, revealing the boy with sapphire eyes that I saw after Eris attacked me. He had a book in his hands and didn't even notice that I was awake. He just walked to the desk and sat down. He marked something in the book and then started sketching on paper.

"Excuse me," I said. "Where am I?"

He jumped off the chair. His face told me that he didn't expect me to be alive. "You're awake?" he asked, confused.

"Yes... how else would I be talking? Believe me! I don't talk in my sleep." I laughed, and the boy seemed to be smiling, but it was more of a forced smile.

"I know. I slept on the corner couch by the window." He pointed at the couch. "Do you want me to help you sit?"

"Yes, please." I tried not to hiss this time because of the pain, but I think I still hissed a little.

My wounds should heel faster than the ones on a human would. That is one of the things I have from being half demon.

"I'm sorry that the bandages aren't put the right way. The ones on the hands are put on by me, while the ones on your stomach are put on by Aunt Roseberry."

I didn't question who was Aunt Roseberry. All I did was be grateful for her bandaging my deep cut.

"I found you a few days ago in the forest," he continued. "My father was at work when I found you. He came home a few minutes after I finished bandaging you."

"You and your Aunt did a great job! Thank you for helping me."

"So, how do you feel? I thought you would not wake up."

"Worst things had happened to me. Much worst..."

I looked around the room to see where my wand could be. I saw my boots but not the wand.

"What's your name?" I asked the boy.

His nose was straight, and his lips puffy. His hair was

covering most of his forehead in the messiest way possible. He seemed around the same age as me but taller.

"My name is Will - actually William. I wouldn't say I like being called William. What about your name?"

"Lili. Actually, Lilium." I said, smiling at the boy.

Will looked like he remembered something important. He went to the desk and took something off it. "This was next to you when I found you." He said and gave me my wand back. "If I didn't know better, I'll say that looks like a wand."

"Because it is," I didn't feel the need to hide this from him. I don't understand why, though. I know what people can do to witches.

"What?"

"It's a wand. See that crystal there?" I showed him where a purple crystal was sitting in the middle of the wand. "That's Amethyst. It's a crystal that is used for protection. I always wear an Amethyst necklace."

"If I didn't know better, I would say that you're a..." he would continue, but I cut him off.

"Witch. Yes, indeed."

"But you don't look like a witch."

"Not every witch is old and ugly. Please, those are just children's bedtime stories."

"So... you're not going to turn me into a frog?"

"Of course not! But I do think you'll make a pretty good chicken," I tried to joke, but he looked at me as if I were about to kill him. "I'm joking. I'm a good witch."

"If you say so, then I believe you." He went to the dresser and took a box from the top. "Here are some clothes that might fit you. They may be a bit big for you, however. Oh, and a tip. Try not to let Dad know you're a witch. He isn't the biggest fan of them."

"I'll try. I haven't had human interactions in years. So it shouldn't be a problem."

He wore a smile on his face. "I'll let you change your bandages. I'm not the best with blood, so If you need anything, I'll be downstairs." I nodded.

He headed to the door.

The wounds were ugly, but Will and Aunt Roseberry cared enough for them so they would not infect. But, for sure, there will be some marks left.

I said my wounds heal faster because of my demon dad, but that doesn't mean they can't infect or leave marks. I have many perks from being half demon, but I also have flaws I don't like discussing. Most of the time, I avoid thinking about being a half-demon. I always concentrate on the witch part of me and never focus on the other part.

The clothes that Will gave me weren't exactly my style, but I can say they were more comfortable than I thought. I am usually the dress and skirt - kind of girl. My mother always gave me pieces out of dresses she made from scraps at work. She used to work for a seamstress. The pieces were big enough for her to make dresses, skirts, or shirts.

The pants he gave me were made of cotton and had the color of walnut wood, and the shirt was a green long-sleeve shirt.

In the box, I also found a piece of ribbon. It was the same color as the shirt, and it looked pretty when I put it in my ginger hair.

After changing, I saw a flash of lightning followed by thunder. Then, water started to pour from the clouds like snow in a snowstorm. If anyone went outside at that moment, the person would come back like ten buckets of water were thrown in their head.

'I am not going back to the meadow today', I thought, but I needed to find Nyx and return to my meadow. I don't feel safe anywhere else.

With Nyx, I feel a connection. I suspect he might be my guide. If he's my guide, that means that he'll always know where I am and that he'll protect me. People who aren't magical have guides, but they call it "humans' best friend".

A guide can be any animal on Earth. For witches, most of the time, are cats, of course.

There is also another big difference between witch guides and human guides. The guide of the witch lives until the witch dies. The guide of human lives until it dies.

The more powerful witches have gods and goddesses as a guide too. Mine's Hecate. Goddess of witchcraft, witches, crossroads, magic, and the moon. She has never been a guide before, yet, she has chosen me. Ever since I was born, I was told that I was the most powerful witch ever born and that I had a big destiny and *blah, blah, blah.* I am sick of being told that all the time. And yes, I am powerful. After all, I am the daughter of a witch and a demon - the first of my kind. I turned out to be more like my mother, but because my father was a demon, my powers amplified, making me even more powerful.

There was also this thing that happened at my birth. My mother's sister is a future-seeing witch, which meant she gave my mother a prophecy that said that I would kill the most powerful demon that ever existed - Eris - that tortured witches worldwide. Everyone expected so much from me and got so little. Everyone I loved died, or I had to leave them behind. So yes, my life is a pain in the ass.

I went out of the room. The hallway had on the walls dark wood paneling on a third of it and then a beige wallpaper with darker flowers that weren't as noticeable from afar, but they were quite beautiful.

A few paintings and family pictures hung in thick wooden frames on the walls.

I walked down the stairs into what I thought is the house's main hallway. The walls had the same wallpaper and paneling. The floors were the same throughout the house; beautiful hardwood floors walnut-colored.

I looked past the big archway and saw Will reading on the couch.

"Did you see a cat near me when you found me in the woods?", I asked him when I came into the room.

"What color was the cat?" he asked, raising his head out of the book. Had I spent that much changing that he had enough time to pick up a book and read? I know how quickly I can pick up a book and start reading it, I have so much free time to spend at the meadow that I am almost every second of the day with a book in my hands. To be honest, when I read a book, it is one of the one hundred and thirty-seven I have in the cabin. I read most of them at least three times.

"Black," I said simply.

"Yes," he said, pointing at the window where a black cat was sitting on the windowsill outside. "He followed me all the way here. He didn't want to leave your side. Is he yours?"

"Yes, he is. His name is Nyx." I went to the window and hugged the cat. Then, I took him and went to sit on the couch with him next to Will.

"If you don't mind, can I ask you a question?" He asked me the moment I sat on the couch. He sat in the corner with the book he was reading in his lap, showing me a serious look.

"Only if I can ask you one, too," I answered.

"Sure."

"Then ask the question." I encouraged him.

"What were you doing in the woods? Why were you in the woods so late? And what happened in the woods?"

"You said a 'question,' not 'some questions', Will."

"My bad," he said with a big smirk on his face that couldn't help but make me smile.

"First of all: I was looking for Nyx," just as I said it, the cat jumped from my lap and sat on the edge of the couch. "Second, I don't have a clock in my cabin, so I didn't know what time it was; I just knew it was late."

He looked like he wanted to ask one more question, but I cut him off. "And third of all: I was attacked by an old enemy."

"And that enemy was...?" he tried getting more answers from me than I allowed him to.

"I think you would run as far away as you can if I told you who it is," I was careful not to use the pronoun *she* because there is only one big bad thing that everyone heard about and uses the pronoun she, and that is Eris. And also, I didn't want to explain why she was my enemy. "My turn now! Why aren't you scared of me?"

"I don't know. I never really believed in magic creatures. To me, they always seemed like bedtime stories. I mean, yeah, it shocked me, but no, I'm not scared. After seeing you, you're not like the witches I heard of - you look nice, and I thought witches should look mean."

"Most witches were hunted by creature hunters and captured, killed, or tortured. And all of..." I thought about some of the witches my mother used to know and corrected myself. "Most of us now are scared to come out of the dark and do what we were born to do - protect the world from evil creatures - because we are afraid that people will find out what we are and kill us," the words came out of my mouth sour and full of pain. "After all, this is how witches live. This is how I live. Every day I live scared of a creature hunter finding me... again..."

I wiped my eyes and nose with the shirt's sleeve. "I just... I... my mom... s-she was killed by a... by a creature hunter." I could barely see through my tears. This was part of the story that was the most sensible, that I tried to ignore.

"You don't have to talk about it if you don't want to."

"I-I think it's best for me to... to talk about it. I'll tell you the short story, to spare you and me for now. I held it in for too long," I took a break before I started the story to find the simpler version. "One day, when I was about eleven, two creature hunters showed up at my house. My mother went to the door to see who it was. I was hiding under the kitchen table and saw the whole thing. The Creature hunters got a dagger and stabbed her in the chest. I got scared and started running out the back door with the creature hunters behind me. I barely escaped."

Will looked shocked. "'I'm sorry' doesn't cover everything. I don't know what to say. You were so young for something like that to happen in front of your eyes."

"Ever since then, I swore that if I found them again, they and Eris would get what they deserved."

"I'm sorry, but did you just say Eris?", said a voice behind me.

Chapter 3

I turned around and saw a tall, dark brown-haired man. His eyes were piercing brown, and his nose was the same shape as his son's. The man's voice was low and silvery.

"I was just telling Lili about some stories from our kingdom." He looked at me like he wanted to say *Play along with this for now.* "Dad, this is Lili; Lili, this is my dad."

"Welcome to our house, Lili! My name is Benjamin." He held out his hand to me, and I shook it. "I thought you'll never wake up."

He walked past the coffee table and turned to Will and me. He stared at me for a while, making me feel uncomfortable. Then, finally, he turned and said to us that he would go and prepare lunch.

Mr. Benjamin went to the door that headed into the kitchen.

"Whatever you do," said Will in a whisper. "Don't speak about Eris. For some reason, he doesn't like people talking about any magical creature, especially Eris."

I laughed. "We have something in common, then."

"Will you tell me about Eris later?" said Will with his voice low, so his father wouldn't hear.

"Yeah... sure..."

He really doesn't care if he talks about her. I don't think he knows anything about her.

"And also, let's not tell her name so often. She has eyes and ears everywhere."

"Got it, Witchy!" I may have blushed at the nickname he gave me, but maybe he didn't see it because of the freckles on my cheeks.

There were a few seconds of silence, maybe even minutes, but it didn't feel weird. Nyx was moving his long tail, tingling my right ear. He was sleeping the same way he sometimes sleeps on my couch or the bed headboard in the cabin.

"Where do you live?" Will asked shyly.

"In a meadow. I don't know how far away from here. I found a cabin there. Far away from where anyone can find me. It's surrounded by woods in which it floods a river. It's quite beautiful. Maybe one day you'll come and visit it."

I asked myself why I told Will everything about me and where I lived. Witches can feel when someone is good and trustworthy. We usually know when something is off, and there was nothing off about Will. I felt like he was the most trustworthy person I had ever met. We usually feel the over roll energy of someone.

After lunch, Will showed me his garden. It was full of flowers and vegetables. In the center was a table, and in the right corner of the garden was a big walnut tree with a swing. There were small roads marked with little rocks the color of sand and Dusty Miller. The air was filled with the smell of rain and wet grass. Finally, the sun started to set. There was a path that went from the picnic table to the gate. In the fence behind the tree, a small gate opened to the neighbor's garden.

I sat on the swing that was surprisingly not wet and started swinging. Will sat at the picnic table.

After all, it was a beautiful evening. But something didn't feel right. Everything seemed way too nice. The birds started singing. From the walnut tree, two blue-greyish birds flew a few centimeters away from my face.

"Is it always like this after it rains here?"

"Most of the time. Why?" he responded.

"Back at the meadow, it rarely rains, and when it does... well... it rains. Like you have thrown a bucket full of water on my head. The witch that lived there before me put some kind of spell on the meadow."

"Do you know the spell? Over here, it rains almost every week."

I saw the way he tried to hide his smirk.

"I wish I knew, Will. So many things were weird when I found the meadow. There were many spell jars, spell books, sour jars, and everything you could think of. I really want to know who lived there. I tried all the things I knew could help me. Time spells, vision manipulation - never trying that again - reading in signs." I said, counting on my fingers. "And many more. Nothing works."

"I'm sure you'll figure it out. And... and do you see that, or is it just me?" He was pointing to something behind me. I slowly turned and saw two figures in the old neighbor's house.

"Shit! Will, get something you can hit them with." The shapes started getting closer and closer.

"Fast!" I yelled.

I took my wand from the boot and tried to make a protection spell. Will went into the back of the house and disappeared.

The shapes started to make it through my spell. At first, I thought the shapes were demons because they were made of black smoke, almost like Eris, but they weren't. Demons can't take the body of an animal. The birds from earlier were the smokes for sure, but I also didn't know what they were either.

Smoke number one tried to get to me from the left, but I made a fire spell and made it get further away from me. Smoke number two approached me from my left and tried to get inside of me, but it just went through me. The smokes looked around, searching for a body to possess.

'Where are you, Will?'

Right on cue, Will came from the opposite side of the one he went to. In his hands, there was a long sword - at least from the waist to the ankle - made of metal. The light from the sun setting was mirroring it, reminding me that it was almost night.

Smoke number two tried to get Will. "Will! Duck! Now!"

He did as I told him, but Smoke number one tried to get him to. Will cut him into two pieces creating Smoke number three. That was the moment I realized what they were.

"Will! They are Shape Spirits. They look for a body to take so they can help the demons. I read about them in a book. If you cut them, you multiply them."

"Then how are we going to destroy them?" He yelled from the other side of the garden.

"We need to find them a host body!"

"And how can we find that?" he said while running next to me.

"If I knew, would they still be here?"

I looked around to see if I could find anything. Smoke number one, followed by Smoke number two, and its child rose to the sky and disappeared.

"Maybe they left because we weren't the ones they were searching for?" Will asked with a hopeful tone.

"I don't think they were searching for someone else."

Like shooting stars, the smoke started flying down with the speed of a fire dragon. "Holy Witch!"

I almost fell over Will. "RUN!"

He looked at the sky, and I saw how his face turned white. Then, he put his sword on his pants belt and ran. We didn't even bother to open the gate. We just jumped over the fence. When I hit the ground, I collapsed from the pain. My wounds weren't even half the way to healing, but here I was, acting like nothing ever happened.

Will helped me to my feet while looking at the Smoke Family. They were close, so we ran faster. The pain was bearable.

We ran through the entire village. The people out of their houses looked at us weirdly, and after they saw that we were followed by smoke thingies and that Will had a sword on his belt, most returned to their houses.

When the stars appeared in the night sky, we were already in the woods, followed by The Smokes. There were so many times when I wanted to stop. The pain was unbearable. For a while, I thought I could manage it, but now I know that running isn't my best idea. I needed to stop every three minutes, but that wasn't an option.

Soon after we entered the woods, I realized we were close to the meadow.

"Will, we're close to the meadow!" I shouted to Will, who was in front of me.

"How... close?" Between the words, he made a pause so he could breathe.

"About ten minutes, maybe. And I might have just the right thing that we could use to kill our smoke friends."

If I had known that the meadow was so close to a village, I wouldn't have stayed there, but now there's no turning back. That's where I feel the safest, where I found Nyx.

My legs turned to stone as if I had just looked into Medusa's eyes.

Nyx. How could I forget him? How could I forget my

best friend? My guide. I am so dumb!

Will ran further. When he saw I wasn't moving, he stopped and looked at me. "Lili, come on!"

"I can't! Nyx is still there!"

"He's safer there than with us right now. Trust me!"

How can I change so much in just a few hours? I went from not trusting anyone, to running with a literal stranger. What the heck is happening to me?

"Let's go before The Smokes get to us," he took my arm and started running. Even if I didn't like the idea of leaving Nyx behind, he was, in fact, safer at Will's house.

The meadow was only a few tens of meters away. Once we entered it, The Smokes would leave us alone, but (yes, there's a *but*) I didn't want to let them free. We needed to get rid of them.

I ran to the shed behind the cabin. "Will, get your sword ready and, at my signal, smash the garden gnomes!"

"Smash the garden gnomes?" He looked at me like I was mad. (I can't blame him.)

I opened the shed door and looked for my three garden gnomes. On the shelves, I put potions and crystals, magical orbs and wands; all that I found, I put there. On the floor, I left multiple boxes filled with herbs and books. Finally, in the corner were my creepy garden gnomes, the ones that haunted me in my dreams. You wouldn't sleep for a week if I told you where I found them. I wanted to get rid of them for so long, and now I got the opportunity to get rid of them.

I took the three nightmare fuels and ran with them to where Will was standing. I put them just a few centimeters away from the magical barrier.

I concentrated. I wanted the gnomes to turn into animals in the eyes of the shape-takers. I pointed my wand at the gnomes and hoped that the spell worked. The smoke charged toward us. They entered the gnomes.

My plan worked.

"Now!" I shouted, and Will smashed the gnomes. They crumbled into small ceramic pieces.

"I never liked them anyway." I collapsed, but Will caught me.

"I think that it's better if we get inside."

Chapter 4

Speaking with a goddess every week makes me lose a lot sleep.

"Are you sure you are fine?" Will asked while we were walking to the cabin uphill.

"Yeah, I'm fine. Those kinds of spells drain me out of power. So I'll be fine in a bit. Don't worry."

As we headed to the cabin, I looked around the meadow. It was the first time in years I had left it. My fruit tree garden was on the right of where we entered it. The back of the meadow was circled by a clear water river.

When we entered the cabin, I went straight to the couch and collapsed. Will sat on the armchair.

"This place is...."

"A mess. Pretty much," I finish the sentence for Will. There were boxes, books, plants, crystals, rocks, cards, bowls, plates, more boxes, and even food everywhere. The cabin was a mess, yet it felt organized to me. At one point, I'll need to take all those things out and deep clean my cabin.

"I wanted to say *nice*, but I guess a *mess* works too." He smiled. "Do you think there is time for us to return to the village?"

"We can go back, but the woods are dangerous at sunset and night, as you can see." I pointed to myself. "I'm going to go make us some hot chocolate. The door to the bathroom is opposite the bed if you need it."

"Thanks." He sat with one hand on the armchair and held his forehead with it. He seemed deep in thoughts. I could feel his worries and stress.

After making the hot cocoa, I put it on my round table and waited for Will to take his. Instead, he rose off the armchair and walked slowly towards the table.

"I think I have a blanket for you in one of the boxes next to the bookshelf."

"He's going to kill me."

"I'm sorry; what did you say?"

"My dad. He's going to kill me when we come back tomorrow."

"Don't be so hard on yourself, Will."

"No, you don't understand. This is the second time I have done something like this. Dad isn't going to be happy about this."

He went to the door. His pants were soaked in blood.

"Will, your leg is bleeding."

He looked at the back of his leg.

"I'll go take the bandages from the bathroom. You should sit on the couch."

I took from the sink's cupboard some bandages and some towels. Then, I washed my hands carefully and went to take care of the wound.

He was sitting on the couch, and he rolled his pant over his knee.

I took one of the towels and applied pressure on his cut.

"Where did you cut your leg?"

"I think with my sword while I was getting you up the hill. It wouldn't be a first," Will said, making me wonder what kind of things he gets himself into.

I took the towel off the cut, and the bleeding stopped. I went to the kitchen sink and wet the other towel I had. With the wet material, I started wiping the blood on the sides of the cut.

"Ahh," sighed Will, looking everywhere but at his leg.

"Aw, come on! It's just a big cut."

"A big cut that hurts."

"That's normal. I'm sure I didn't complain that much when you took care of my wounds."

"You were unconscious!" he added, and we both chuckled.

After I cleaned the cut and took the bandage, I wrapped it around the part of the leg that had the wound on it.

"It's unnecessary to put bandages on it, but I think it will be better for now. You can take it down in the morning."

"How are your wounds?"

"Better, I think," I said with no life in my voice. "Like, it hurt more at the beginning when I woke up."

"You've been asleep for almost a week; I think it is normal."

Geez, a week; why doesn't this surprise me? After all, it was Eris. "I think the cut on my stomach might leave me with a scar."

When I finished wrapping Will's cut, I went and washed the spots of blood that were left on my hands.

After I gave Will a blanket, we hung around for a bit, then decided to sleep. He fell asleep almost as soon as his head touched the couch pillow. I, on the other hand, didn't fall asleep as quickly.

The wind outside was blowing the leaves of the trees and made the sweet sound of the night. It helped me relax.

After just a few minutes, Will started to snore. He was lying on his back with one hand on the side of the couch.

His blanket was on the not-so-clean floor.

Some minutes passed, and I decided to meditate. I sat cross-legged on the bed. I closed my eyes and emptied my mind, which was more complicated than usual. But when I managed it, my body and mind were at peace. My mind cleared, and my body relaxed. A soft breeze of wind crept through the window, all around me, and stopped at my head.

"Hecate," I said softly. "A pleasure as always."

On the edge of the bed, a tall women appeared. My guide had long black hair that touched the bed sheets. She wore a long black dress with long puffy black sleeves made of vail. On her forehead sat a silver diadem that pictured a full moon and two half-moons - one of her symbols.

"Why don't we go for a walk?" She gave me her hand, and I took it. I stepped out of my body. I looked back at it. Sitting so peacefully, like I was asleep, but in reality, I was walking with the goddess of magic herself.

It seemed like a dream for me that I was trained by a goddess. I always needed to pinch myself to know that I wasn't dreaming.

The night got cooler than when we went inside, but it was still warm for a spring day.

"To what do I owe this pleasure?" I let a whisper come out of my mouth.

"I saw a glimpse of the future with the help of my cousin Apollo. Nothing to worry about for now, my dear, but I should warn you. The time will come soon. What happened earlier is only a fraction of what Eris has up her sleeves. The smallest fraction."

"But that's not why you came," I said simply.

Her glittery purple eyes - a few shades darker than mine - looked at me scared. Maybe a part of regret. Sadness? Fear?

Hecate stopped at the side of the river. The wind blew her long hair, leaving no strand in her face. I stepped next to her and looked at the trees.

"A choice," she said like a soft breeze. "In the future. About that boy."

I choked. "You mean Will?"

"You felt a connection with him, didn't you? What if I told you that connection could put the world in danger? Your world."

"I... I-I just met him."

"And yet you feel like you can trust him with your life."

"That's not... That's not what I... I haven't had any human interaction in three years." I protested.

"I might not be human, but you have talked to me."

Touché.

"You should let your feelings out sometimes. You might not know, but when you talked about your mother's death, you started healing mentally," she pointed to my head. "You didn't talk much about it, but you talked. He will help you more if you allow him to. Just believe in what your feelings tell you to do."

She stood there looking at the trees for as long as it took me to ask her a question. "You know what Eris's plan is?"

"I know and not know. But, if I told you, the end result wouldn't be the same." She looked at the hill where I star gazed. "Come with me, my dear witch."

She lifted her dress and started walking up the hill. Even if she could teleport herself up there, it was nice for her not to use it and walk with me.

She sat on the blanket I always have set there.

"You two will push each other to your limits and over. This world isn't big enough for you." She pointed at the stars. "Your story got told all across the universe. It's only at the start. You should understand that this is the life you have. You may fall, break, and get lost, but you'll get stronger. You may not have chosen this life, but this life chose you for a reason."

She seemed to talk for someone else. To me, those words didn't seem to align in the way they were supposed to. She said things so clearly even a child would understand, but to me, they seemed like a puzzle she wanted me to solve.

"You have an entire life before you, so don't be scared to live it. You're one in a million."

We didn't say anything for a couple of good minutes. The silence was uncomfortable, making me want to return to the cabin, but I didn't leave. She wouldn't be so happy if I went before Hecate told me to.

"Now look at that star," she pointed at a more golden than white star. "That's your mother. Make her proud."

I looked at it. Part of me didn't believe that was her, while the other part was reassured that my mother was still watching me after all this time.

"Now I think it's time for me to leave." She started to dissolve into small particles of glitter, and I was left alone next to a puddle of glitter. I felt a slight shock which meant I was back in my body.

I didn't leave the cliff. I changed spots. Laid on my back. Walked by the river. The only thing I didn't do was go back inside. I could only think of the things that Hecate said. A choice about Will. A connection with him. We'll push each other to the limits and over.

I kept looking at the top of the trees where the nature spirits were floating. Then, the sky started to color in multiple shades of pink and yellow. The birds began to sing. I don't know for how long I sat there. The time flew by so fast that it felt like just a few minutes. The pile of glitter was spread all the way to the side of the hill and on the flowers.

I knew I had stood up all night when I saw a shadow in front of the kitchen window looking at me. The cabin door opened, and Will came out and walked to me. I don't want him to know about any of the things that Hecate said to me. I don't want him to know that I even talked to her. (Is because I don't know how to explain to him that I speak to a goddess weekly.)

He sat next to me and looked in the direction I was looking. "Why is glitter all over the cliff?" he looked at me funny.

"Hard to explain." I tried to joke.

"Have you been up all night?"

"No. Why?" I said too fast.

"I woke up a few hours ago and didn't see you. So I went back to sleep, and you still weren't there when I woke up. So you were up here all night."

"You are a good detective."

"Thanks. The training helps."

"Training?" I looked at him, confused.

"My dad sends me every few weeks to the castle to

train. You know, sword fight and stuff. I want to become a royal guard. The sword that I used was my mom's. She also wanted to become a guard. They didn't let her train because she was a girl."

"Girls can do things as well as boys can ," I argued with him.

"That, I can agree with. But that's not the idea. She trained with her father - my grandpa - who retired, and after a few years, she went to a contest held at the castle. She was the only girl there. That caught my dad's eye. She fought the toughest men in the kingdom and won. The king himself hired her to be the head guard. She died in battle almost five years ago."

"Then she looks over you every second of your life."

"What do you mean."

"She's a star. She will always look at you. No matter day or night."

"How do you know that?"

"I just do," I told him, looking at the glitter on the green grass and then at the sky and smiling. "I just do."

Chapter 5

My witch brain will never have enough crystals.

"We should be out of the woods in just a bit," I reassured Will.

"You said that five minutes ago too," Will noticed, and I rolled my eyes.

We were walking in a wood clearing close to the village. Will lost hope and said that we were lost forever. We walked in a circle, looking for an exit from this mess.

Now I decided to go right instead of left, and we went out of the woods and found ourselves next to the village. All we had to do was find Will's house, and I was counting on him for that.

"Now we should be at my house in a bit, Flower," he joked. Ever since we left the cabin, he started calling me *Flower.* I thought it was sweet of him.

An old woman waved to him on the street near Will's house.

"Will, where have you been? Your father is searching for you. Oh, hello, young lady," the woman said, looking at me sweetly. Her eyes were the color of almonds and also had the shape of one. Her face was baggy, and her hair was as silver as the moon. She had chocolate skin and was so much shorter than Will and short compared to my height.

"Aunt Roseberry, this is Lili. Lili, this is Aunt Roseberry."

"Beautiful name," she smiled at me, and I returned the smile. She gave me a weird feeling. Not bad. Just weird.

"You two should head back. Your father won't be happy." She turned to Will.

"Yeah, I think so. See you later!"

"Goodbye, Will. Goodbye, Lili."

We waved at her and walked further. I looked back at her and saw a black cat rubbing around her feet. Was that Nyx, or was I having visions?

"I think your aunt is a witch."

"She is not really my aunt. She used to take care of me, and I called her aunt, and it remained like that. And I don't really think she's a witch. I would've noticed for sure if she was."

"If you say so. But I still think she's a witch."

"Of course you do," he said playfully.

He was so happy and relaxed, like he wouldn't soon get punished by his dad. Maybe Hecate was right. Opening up to people can help you.

On the street, everyone waved at Will and looked weird at me. I didn't blame them. Redhead, purple eyes, full of freckles, and hands and legs bandaged.

Where I used to live, I was treated very poorly. I was the only one who had red hair. My mother didn't have it. She had long golden brown locks. So every time I went out, the people on the street started calling me ugly names that I tried to forget. Some of them have stayed with me ever since and will always stay. They lived by the stereotype of all redheads being robbers, traitors, and evil witches.

With every year I took in age, the names got worse. They appeared even in my cousin's village every time I went there.

They wouldn't stop. After a while, I stopped going out on the streets. I would only go into the garden, where there were tall fences.

As we got closer to the house, I got anxious. What if he saw me? What if he knows I'm a witch? What if he told the entire village, and now they're going to light me up?

Stop it, Lili! Everything's going to be all right. You need to calm down, I told myself.

Nothing was *all right.*

Will's dad was fuming mad.

"What in the living heck were you thinking, Will?" yelled Benjamin. "Running away. With a *witch*."

I was sitting so ashamed in the corner of the couch. Will's dad stood in front of us on the other side of the coffee table, lecturing us that we shouldn't have run from the village. (Read as "lecturing Will that he shouldn't have let me kidnap him.")

"First time you ran from the castle from your training, and now you ran from home who knows where! Are you out of your mind?" he yelled at his son, then turned to face me. "What do you want from us?"

"I-I don't want anything. I got lost in the woods and then attacked by..."

"Attacked by what? By Eris. Do you think I believed Will's little excuse? Who are you, and what do you want from us?"

"Dad," Will tried to warn him.

Benjamin showed Will a face that made him not say another word.

All the anger piled up. I needed to relax, so I took a deep breath and said. "I'm Lili Grace. And yes, I'm a witch. And I don't want anything from you."

"You think I believe you?"

"Dad, just listen to her. She's telling the truth," Will broke the silence given by his dad.

Benjamin went into the kitchen and stood there looking through the window.

Nor Will nor I dared to speak. We just looked at the kitchen and at each other. When he came back, he looked sad.

"Look, here is what going to do," he spoke in a calmer tone. "In two weeks, I'm taking you to the castle. The king will see you. If the king says you can remain in the kingdom, that's good for you. If he doesn't, there are two things he might do to you. First, he'll get you out of the kingdom, never able to return. Second is that he'll put you in a prison cell and let you there until he knows what to do with you."

I listened carefully to his words, trying to find any trap. Anything that might not be true in his words. I repeated his words in my mind, finding no lie.

"And also, until then, you'll stay here with us. Just to be sure I'm not making a mistake by bringing you to the castle and not sending a letter to the castle to bring some guards here," he added when he saw I was about to speak.

My hands froze. I looked into his eyes to see if he was real. I couldn't leave my meadow for a week, return for one night, leave it for two weeks again, and then return who knows when.

"Sounds good?"

I accepted, even though I didn't want to. I didn't want to lose my new friend... and probably my life too.

"I think your dad let me loose," I told Will when he came from downstairs.

"He definitely did. At least much looser than me." He sat on the chair at his "desk." It was made out of two shelves placed next to each other. "Two weeks of training with no free day. Jokes on him, I actually like training. So he didn't really punish me."

I turned to look out of the window on the hexagonal couch. I can see the entire village from up here, even to the furthest house. Kids played outside, and adults took care of their gardens. In the center of the village, there was some kind of fest.

"You have a beautiful view from here."

"I'm the only one who sees it." He explained to me. "This is the tallest house in the village, and it's also on the top of a hill. My dad doesn't see this view. He can see the garden from his room window."

"Your garden is beautiful."

"Yours too."

"Mine is a living mess," I said, amused. "Literally," I gave one more look at the view. "Is there some kind of fest over there?"

"No. This is how every day is. Today's kind of busy. We can go there in the next few days if you want."

"I'll be happy if we did. Now I think that I need to change. Do you know where my dress is?"

"Yeah, about that," he said, scratching the back of his neck. "Your dress is kind of teared apart. We can look in the attic for some that were my mom's if that's ok with you."

"I don't have any other choice," I told him while heading to the door.

He followed me and opened a trap door in the ceiling, taking out a ladder. He went first, and I went only after he was in the attic. To be clear, I was skeptical about the ladder.

The attic was half of Will's height - about eighty-five centimeters. It was full of boxes and old toys. And a lot of wooden swords. A small window seemed to open and lead to the roof. On the oblique walls of the roof, there were all kinds of drawings and old pictures.

"I think the clothes should be over there," Will said, pointing on his knees at the corner or the attic. The darkest, scariest corner of the attic. Of course. Where else could they be?

There were a lot of things that caught my eye.

There was an entire library here. I saw at least ten boxes on which was written BOOKS.

"Dad keeps all of Mom's stuff in the back so that he doesn't have to see them whenever he comes here."

He didn't seem to be telling me those things. Instead, it seemed like he was saying it more to reassure himself.

Will took one of the boxes and gave it to me. "In here, there should be some shirts, pants, and socks." Then he gave me another box. "And here, there should be two dresses and other things."

I put them down next to me and looked at the pile of boxes. On each of them was written something. Then, at the back of them, I saw something shining.

"What's that?"

Will moved some of the boxes to the side, revealing a collection of crystals almost as big as mine. Immediately my witch mind went:

Crystals. Give them to me.

"Look! That's an emerald," I pointed at a green crystal,

and then at a red one. "And that's a ruby. And that blue one is a sapphire." I picked it up and showed it to him.

"It kind of looks like your eyes," I added, and I saw a blush on Will's face in the dim light. "Can I take it? I don't have one in my collection."

"Yeah. I don't do anything with it. They just stay here collecting dust. You can take them all if you want."

I almost hit my head on the ceiling out of excitement. I hugged Will to thank him. "Thank you so, so, so much."

"You're welcome, Flower," he said, hugging me back.

His hair smelled like a pine tree and rainwater - two of my favorite smells - and was softer than mine could ever be. His hands touched the ends of my untied hair, but I froze when he touched my back. This was the best moment to remember what Hecate said. I pulled out of the hug and tried to cover my face with the grown bangs I had cut months ago.

Was I blushing?

"Do you," I broke the silence, "have a box or something in which I can put the crystals?"

"Yes. I think there are some cardboard boxes in the box behind you."

"You keep boxes in boxes?" I giggled.

"Yeah. Wasn't my idea."

After we put all the crystals in a box, Will went down the ladder, and I started passing him the boxes.

Chapter 6

Families can be complicated.

Two weeks far away from the meadow. At least I'm with Nyx.

Will and I got closer. We became best friends immediately. His dad warmed up a little bit to me, just a little tiny bit.

Four days had passed since the time we were in the attic. I slept on the couch in Will's living room. I wasn't wearing bandages anymore on my arms and legs. I only had one on my stomach. The clothes we found in the attic were comfortable. The dresses were clearly worn only once or twice. Today I wore the light green one with a chessboard pattern and my boots.

I was sitting on the chair at Will's desk, with my head on my hands, looking through a transparent crystal. It projected small rainbows all around the room. Nyx was sitting on the bed with his legs up, sleeping. Will was helping his dad cook something because his grandparents and aunt (real aunt) were coming later today. I would've helped them, but Will's dad told me they didn't need help (in a nice way) - I guess he still didn't trust me enough.

I sat and thought. I never should've accepted to stay here for two weeks. I needed to go to the meadow and check it. But if I went to it alone without them knowing, they (Will's dad) would think I ran away because I was evil. But still, the temptation was there.

I heard a loud snort, and I jumped out of the chair. Looking around, I saw a book on the ground and Will standing in the door frame.

"What the heck, Will?"

He had a big smirk on his face that told me he was proud of what he did. "I called you for a whole minute, and you didn't respond, so I did the next best thing." He pointed at the book on the ground.

"Well, you could've patted me on the shoulder."

"This was more fun. Anyway. I think we should go down. My grandparents are here, and they want to meet you."

"The fact that people wanna meet me is something I'll never get used to."

"Just wait till you go to the castle."

"I don't like how that sounds."

"Don't worry; the people of Lovskaria are the nicest in the seven kingdoms. Shall we go down now?"

I went next to him and told him in a whisper. "We shall

see if the people like me."

I walked past him to the stairs. I took one more look at him and saw how stunned he looked in the door frame. I giggled to myself.

When I reached the middle of the stairs, Will joined me.

"They're outside," he said.

We both put our shoes on and went to the kitchen. Will took a plate with meat and potatoes from the counter and stepped out the door. They were talking with Will's dad. His grandmother had short silvery hair and a petite figure. On the other side, his grandad had "salt and pepper" hair and a tall, robust figure. His aunt had long brown hair, half up, half down, and a tall but slim body.

I walked in the shadow of Will. I sat down next to his aunt. She didn't seem to have more than twenty-something years. His grandparents seemed to have around sixty.

"Nice to meet you," I said with a smile. "I'm Lili."

"I'm Lydia. And those are my parents, Amara and Lincoln." She said, giving me her hand to shake. Her parents nodded, and we started eating.

I ate some potatoes. I tried eating some meat but haven't eaten any in years. To be honest, I missed its taste.

They talked about family stories and other stuff. I barely

said a word. Will tried to make me talk, but I just felt like a pink lily in a garden full of yellow ones.

I discovered that Benjamin would leave for a few days for his job at the castle. Maybe I can convince Will to go with me to the meadow.

"I really like your neckless," said Lydia. "It's so pretty."

"Oh, thank you. It's amethyst."

"From where did you get it?"

"I made it." I smiled.

"Don't you remember, Lydi," interrupted Amara. "Your sister used to make those too. She had a whole collection of crystals and books about them."

"I do remember that," said Lydia with a half-smile.

"But she didn't die with crystals around her neck. Nyota died with honor. As a warrior," announced Lincoln.

"She was more than that, Dad," protested Lydia.

"Why don't we a... finish dessert?" Will tried to defuse the situation.

I could feel the tense connection between Lydia and her father. They didn't seem to get along that great. Family drama, what can I say?

We ate the lemon tart Will's grandmother made. It was delicious but not as good as the one my mother used to make.

"How did you get here, Lili?" asked Will's grandfather.

My mind started thinking of a lie to say. I saw from the corner of my eye how Will's expression changed; he probably thought about a lie too.

I was the one to tell it first, "I got lost in the woods. Wolves attacked me, and Will found me."

It was simple and easy to believe, and Will's family seemed to buy it.

They didn't ask any other questions about me and my past, which was great. I didn't wanna tell them about it. Will's grandparents didn't give me the best feeling, but his aunt gave me a different feeling.

They talked about Will's training and different techniques he could try. Finally, they asked about Benjamin's travels.

At one point, I said I needed to go to the bathroom to escape the feeling of being ignored.

I went inside and walked the stairs. When I got to the door of Will's room, the crystal I was looking at before caught my eye again.

Now that the sun filled the room with light, the crystal reflected even more rainbows around the room. I immediately thought about how it would look with even more crystals in the light.

I thought about not doing it but fell prey to the temptation.

I took the box and put on the floor all of the crystals. Then, I put each of the crystals in direct sunlight.

With every crystal put in, the room had even more color.

Every step I took had to be careful so as not to step on any of them. They were everywhere.

When I placed the last one, I closed my eyes and walked to the door, afraid not to walk on one of the crystals.

I turned so that when I opened my eyes, I would face the room, not the hallway.

As I opened my eyes, I laughed with delight. The room was soaked with the light of the sun and the colors that came from the crystals.

It made me think of the spells my mother used to make for me before sleep, but the ones she made were during the night. It looked like a day wonderland.

"When did you had time to do this?" asked the voice of Lydia.

I turned to see her standing in the door frame, her long hair making a curtain behind her back. "To say, I didn't need to go to the bathroom." My response didn't seem right for the question, but it was the only one I could think of.

"I understand. My parents aren't the best at making people comfortable around them." She came near me and looked through the room, her eyes fixing on my dress. "From where did you get the dress?"

"Will didn't have that many options to give me." I tried to joke. "He said it was his mother's."

"I knew it!" she said with a tint of melancholy. "I remember when she wore it. Only once. When we went to our grandparents. They didn't like the idea of Nyota becoming a knight."

"It's a really nice dress. Comfortable too."

"It was her favorite."

She took a pause, maybe thinking about her sister. I remember how much I thought about my mother and still think about her. Most people seem to get over losing someone they loved easier than others, but there are still the ones who will always think about their lost one.

"I like what you did here," she said, walking to the crystal I put in the window. "Never saw Will's room with so many colors in it. Always blues, beiges, and browns. Maybe you can make Will add more color to it. It always looks boring in here."

I laughed.

"It's been ages since I saw these crystals last." She was looking at the transparent one.

"Will gave them to me. If you want, you can take them,"

I said and saw the surprise on her face. "They were your sisters, after all."

"Will gave them to you, not to me."

I moved, so I was sitting by the desk. Looking at Lydia, I could see the similarities between her and Will. They shared the same hair color, that light chocolaty brown. However, Lydia's eyes weren't the same bright sapphire blue as Will's. They were more desaturated - more grey than blue - with a black circle around them and dark gray flakes in them.

"I only want the sapphire," I said, touching the blue crystal. "You can take all of the others. I already have more than enough crystals at home."

"My parents won't be happy if I take them. They didn't like that part of her."

"Why?"

The moment I said that, I already regretted it. I saw the change in her face and her body language. She bit her lip and put a strand of hair behind her year.

"I don't know. After she started training to become a guard, all my parents could see in her was that. I saw more in her. My big sister raised me and taught me about life when my parents didn't. I knew her best, yet I didn't know everything about her.

She had secrets she kept with her life. Secrets that brought her to her death. I'll never know what they were; I'm sure no one else will. They will sleep with her forever."

Chapter 7

Time passed by, and it was a few days before I was going to meet the king. Will offered to take me to the center of the village so I could see what was around.

We were walking on the street that led to the center of the village, where the town's folks had some stalls. Nyx was sitting on my shoulders, looking all around us. I was wearing a brown skirt, a flowery white puffy-sleeved dress, and brown leather boots.

The street was full of children playing. Everyone was happy and taking care of everything. People were cleaning windows and painting their houses. Some were cutting the grass, and others were feeding animals. Everyone was all smiles and laughs. They put me in a better mood. For all the years I lived in my old village, not a single day was like this one. In the village I used to live with my mother, everyone was scared to do anything. To be true, our village was full of dangerous people and evil witches and creatures. So no one really dared to go out and do stuff. I was one of the only kids who actually played outside. Most of the parents didn't let their kids out, so I used to go out and play with the rabbits that used to come into our garden. I could see the neighbors looking at me through the windows like I was crazy. People barely went out on the streets, whereas in Will's village, people were everywhere.

A little girl with golden hair came to me and gave Will and I a daisy. I put mine in my hair and thanked her. She went blushing back to her friends.

"The people here are really nice," I said.

"The people all around Lovskaria are nice. I wonder why the ones in your old village weren't. You sure you are from Lovskaria?"

"I genuinely don't know. I barely remember what my village was named. It's like that memory was erased. I only remember how the village was and its people. No name, no kingdom. I only remember they hated witches."

"You know, there's no law against witchcraft in this kingdom. There are some really big witches - good witches - in our kingdom's history. If anything, witches are friends of us."

"Then why does your dad hate me?" I asked.

"He doesn't hate you. He just... I don't know, Lili. But I'm sure he doesn't hate you."

"Some people don't have a reason, Sapphires." He smiled at his nickname while I remembered the crystals we found in the attic that I later gave to his aunt. "I usually can feel the overall vibe of a person, but your dad is hard to read."

"Was I easy to read?", he asked.

"Kinda. I felt you were a good person and a lovely soul. Just nice, overall." I smiled, and he did the same.

I thought for a second. "If witchcraft isn't illegal, then why does your dad want me to see the king?"

"Witchcraft might not be illegal, but when someone meets a witch, that person has to go with the witch to the castle and check if the witch is good." He responded to my unsaid question when I wanted to interrupt him. "No matter if the witch didn't do anything bad, she is obligated to go to the king with the person that found her."

"That would be you," I added.

"That would be me. You're right, but my dad will never let me go alone before the king. He'll probably say *he* found you; I was just there doing something else and didn't see you. Or something along those lines."

"That would mean that he'll lie in front of the king. That's not right."

"You'll be surprised how much he lied in front of him."

We got to the center of the village, and I looked around. It had some stalls and small shops. I was still thinking about seeing the king. Will probably felt what I thought because he knew what to say.

"Don't worry about the king," he said. "He's a nice guy. He never did something bad to a witch. Trust me?"

"I trust you, but... but I don't trust the king. And neither your dad. Sorry."

"Don't blame you. If I were you, I wouldn't trust him either," he laughed, then pointed at a stall where Miss Roseberry stood. "Why don't we go say 'Hi' to her?"

The old lady was sitting on a chair in the back of a stall. She was reading a book with the word "History" and some other words on the cover. I don't want to be mean, but she looks ancient enough to know most of the kingdom's history. Nyx jumped off my shoulders and went to Roseberry's feet.

"Hello, little kitty," she said, patting him on his head. He started purring at the women's feet. She took Nyx and put him in her lap. Then she rose her head and smiled at us. Her almond color eyes changed for a second to bright green and blue and then back to almond. Her dark skin shone in the light of the sun.

"Hello, dears. With what can I help you?"

"Aunty Roseberry, I didn't know you had a stall."

"Of course I have. And it's full of the things I love," she looked at the table full of crystals, necklaces, bracelets, and flowers. "I have to do something with my free time since I don't babysit you anymore," the woman joked.

I looked at the things she had on her table; a hand full of great crystals and some charming necklaces and bracelets. Next to the table, there were two buckets full of flowers.

"They're from my garden, dear. Aren't they beautiful?"

"I bet your garden is flawless if those flowers look like this."

"I had a garden even more beautiful than I have now." She said dreamily. "It had fruit trees and a river and even more flowers."

"It sounds beautiful."

"It was, and I bet it still is." She looked down under the table. "Oh, I forgot to put those on the table."

She placed on the table some boxes with what seemed like a deck of cards in them.

"So, any of those things interest you?" she asked.

Will nudged me in the shoulder with his.

"I-I really like the moonstone neckless."

"Good choice. Moonstones are great for protection."

"It's a crystal that soothes and calms its wearer by dispelling cosmic fog and negative energy," I continued. "It's known for karmic healing. The Moonstone has been used as a protective talisman for travelers for generations. It's known to aid focus and awareness and even enhance psychic powers."

"You're a smart girl. Anything else you might like?"

"I think the cards are beautiful. The box has really pretty drawings on it. Is this how they look?"

She took the cap off the box and put the cards on the table. They had almost a watercolor look to them, for sure handmade. The queen looked almost like Hecate, but the king looked nothing like a god, and I met a few.

"They're gorgeous."

"They are painted by my granddaughter, Willow. She's about your age," she said with a sweet voice.

"How much are the neckless and the deck of cards?" asked Will.

I looked at Will, stunned. "Will, you don't have to."

"But I will."

"Will, really, you don't have to. You don't have to buy them for me."

"They're four silver coins, dear," interrupted Aunt Roseberry.

Will put on the old women's table four silver coins. "Thank you."

"See you two around," she said as we started walking. "Oh, and Will. You should take Lili to the festival in the center on the princess's birthday."

We were a little outside the village, walking around. Then, we took a break to rest. We were sitting under a big tree. I was sitting on the grass while Will sat on a rock. It was really hot. I could hear a river nearby.

The grass was green and full of small white flowers.

"What was the festival Roseberry was talking about?"

"In two months is the princess's sixteen birthday, and there is a festival in her honor," he explained.

"Can we go to it?"

"I guess we can."

The place where we were sitting reminded me deeply of my meadow. Most days, I sat just like I sat under a tree, reading, practicing magic, and doing everything I wanted to. God, I miss my meadow!

"Do you want to help me with a spell?" I asked him. "It's actually not a spell, it's more like a... I don't know."

"Sure."

"Really?"

"Yeah. I'll help you."

"Oh, cool." Part of me didn't believe that he actually wanted to help me. "Ok, so, the day before you found me in the woods... I tried to learn to access the memories I lost when I got to the meadow. But I needed first to be able to access someone else's memories. It usually is the other way, but this spell is different. Do you still want to help me?"

I looked at his face to see if he had changed his answer.

"I'll help you," he responded. "I trust you."

"Okay. Come and stay in front of me."

He got up and sat on the grass in front of me.

"Is this going to hurt?" He looked into my eyes with his sapphire ones.

"No, it won't. Shall we start?"

He nodded. I told him to put his hands on top of mine. I concentrated on his touch. I closed my eyes and tried to feel a connection. A slight tingle in my hands made me open my eyes.

I was back in the woods. It was lighter than the time I met Eris. I looked at my hands. They were Will's.

I was walking through some bushes, saw a weird stick, and picked it up. It was *my* wand. I walked a few more meters and saw a body covered in blood.

A fun part of this spell is that I can feel what Will felt at

the moment, which was quite an abundance of feelings...
and also vomit. Happily, I didn't vomit. But I could barely
look at the body. So I moved closer to see if I was breathing.

"Oh my goodness gracious! What do I do now?" I yelped.

I picked up the body (and may I say I'm quite light) and
tried not to vomit because of the amount of blood.

"Lili," I heard a voice from somewhere else, out of the
vision.

I kept walking. The air got a little colder. Black smoke
swirled around me. I could've think it was a bird - it
probably seemed so to Will - but I knew it was Eris. She
laughed as she had just won.

"Lili," I heard Will's voice again.

I was almost out of the woods when I woke, lying on the
grass in the warm sun.

Will looked at me, worried. "B-blood started running
from your nose."

"Shit."

"Language."

I pinched the soft part of my nose above my nostrils,
lending foreword and breathing through my mouth.

"What happened?"

"I'll explain it to you in a bit. Let me just... let me just finish this," I said, exhausted, still pinching my nose.

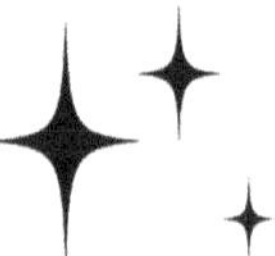

After a while, the nosebleed stopped. Will went to get me some water. I was lying with my head resting on the tree. I didn't know that those kinds of things take so much energy. I felt like I ran for hours with no break.

Gosh, wish Hecate would've told me this before. She never tells me the whole thing. Never lets me see the complete spell. Most of the time, I knew half of the truth. She hid my memories of my old village and childhood. When I asked her to do that, I didn't ask her to leave me with only the sad parts. I was left remembering only the bad stuff. I had only a few happy memories, which weren't that great. That's all I had of my childhood. Cruel, sad memories. Why did she leave me with only those?

I was so angry that purple smoke was coming out of my fingertips.

I started shaking my hands to make the fume go away. I tried relaxing.

Next to me appeared a glass water bottle without a lid.

"Oh, my God! Thank you. I feel like I haven't drank water in days."

"What happened?" He looked worried.

I bit the inside of my cheek. "The vision took more power than I expected."

He thought for a second, then said. "At the meadow, your nose didn't bleed. So why didn't it bleed?"

"Back at the meadow, I channeled less power than now, even though what I did now was simpler. It's magic; it's weird." I wished we would stop talking about this; it would only make me angrier and more stressed. But he didn't stop.

"What did you see?"

"The moment you found me in the woods."

"Why did you see that memory?"

"God, Will, I don't know?" I said, frustrated.

"But... From where did you learn this?" He said, a little scared.

"Why are you asking all these questions?" I yelled at him. "Please, just stop! Why do you care so much about it?"

"Lili, I..." He looked scared. No, no, no, no. Not this. Why do I scare everyone?

"Your hands are fuming a purple haze," he ended.

I jumped up and started shaking, hoping the fumes would

go away. They didn't, and that only made things worse. I started panicking. I couldn't think clearly.

Hello, my dear. However, it will be a long time till we meet again.

"Get. Out. Of. MY. Head, Eris!" I screamed. My eyes became watery. The fumes started covering my entire body.

Let me in. You know it's hopeless. You can't control it.

"You don't know me!"

I know you better than you know yourself.

The fumes became fire and started to spread around me. I was scared. Eris knows that my weakest moments are the best ones to try to take control over me. She knows that if I lose control, nothing is holding her back. If I lose control, I lose myself.

"Lili. Listen to me." I heard Will. His voice was insecure and shaking. "I know you're scared... and so am I."

"You don't get it, don't you? That's exactly what I don't want." I cried. "I don't want people to be scared of me."

"I know you don't. Nobody wants that." He looked at me, understanding. "Try taking control of it. You don't have to nail it on the first try. You just have to try. That's all you have to do. Try."

My tears felt like fire on my face. I didn't want Eris

taking control. I didn't want to scare more people.

I closed my eyes and tried to get Eris out of my mind.

Get out. I told her.

I may leave you for now, but it won't be forever, she responded.

GET OUT!

No response. She was out, and I managed to retain control of myself. The only remining fire was at my fingertips. I shook my hands, and it disappeared. To my surprise, I wasn't exhausted. But I was shaking and crying, and I was scared for my life.

Will came closer to me. I grabbed and hugged him for dear life, crying on his shoulder.

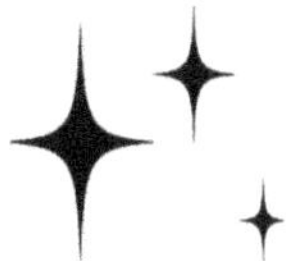

I was sitting under the tree in Will's garden. The sun was setting. I told Will I wanted some time alone. He was packing for the two weeks of training.

I sat cross-legged, shuffling the cards Will gave me today to cleanse them. When they felt cleansed, I did a one-card reading for myself. Then, not too far into shuffling, a card flew out of the deck. I looked to see what it was. Ace of Hearts. I blushed slightly.

"This can't be right," I told myself while reshuffling the cards.

Every time a card flew out of the deck, I looked to see what it was. Every time it was Ace of Hearts.

When I decided to do the reading, it was the same card as the one that kept flying away.

"Maybe it's right after all."

Chapter 8

This night, right before I leave for the castle, the sky will be full of falling stars.

I remember I sat on top of my hill last year, watching the stars all alone. Nyx didn't want to come out of the cabin. I was lucky that night. The sky was brighter than ever. No clouds. I saw the stars perfectly that night and I hope it will be the same tonight.

The last meteor shower I saw with my mother, we sat on the roof of our house, eating the cookies my mother had made earlier that day. She held me close to her and made me laugh at all the things she told me about the falling stars and the Greek stories. She never told me the tragic part. She made up her own ending, even though she knew that I was aware of the real one.

Will told me that we could watch the meteor shower on the roof of his house. So I went there earlier and watched the sunset.

The few clouds in the sky turned orange, while the sky turned a cold blue. Then, the sky took a purple mask as the sun went further to the other side of the earth. Finally, the orange clouds became pink.

When the sun went down, and the sky turned dark blue, Will came and sat next to me on the roof.

"You got to see the sunset?" He gave me a bowl with fruits and cookies in it.

I nodded lightly. "But you came at the right moment." I pointed at a falling star.

After a while, I started pointing out constellations to Will and telling the story of them to him.

"And that's the Capricorn," he said. "Right?"

"Yeah."

"I'm a Capricorn. I was born on the twenty-second of December."

"So you're turning sixteen this year," I said as he nodded. "Do you want to know the story behind it?"

"Sure."

Did he actually wanted to hear it? By his response, I didn't get the vibe that he wanted. Of course, he might want to listen to me tell the story out of politeness. But, on the other hand, he might not even want to be on the roof looking at the stars with me.

Stop it, Lili! You're overthinking it!

I shrugged. "The Greeks associated the constellation

with Pan, the forest deity, who had legs and horns like a goat. He was a satyr.

His son, Crotus, is usually associated with another creature, represented by another constellation - Sagittarius.

Pan was placed in the sky by Zeus in gratitude for his coming to the other gods' rescue on several occasions. During the gods' war with the Titans, Pan helped scare the Titans away by blowing his conch shell. Later, he warned the gods that Typhon - a monster sent by Gaea to fight them - was approaching. He also suggested that gods disguise themselves as animals until the danger passed."

I looked at him to see if he was following me. I could feel the question he was about to ask me, so I answered it before he asked it. "Gaea is the personification of the Earth."

He nodded and told me to continue telling the story.

"In the myth, Pan eluded the monster himself by jumping into the river Nile and turning the lower part of his body into the body of a fish. Eventually, Zeus struck down Typhon with his thunderbolts. Capricornus is still often depicted as a goat with the tail of a fish.

In another story, Capricornus is identified as Amalthea, the goat that suckled Zeus when he was an infant, hiding from his father, Cronos. Cronos had devoured his other children, all future gods and goddesses, because of a prophecy that said he would be overthrown by one of them."

"What is your zodiac sign?"

"Gemini." I didn't ask if he wanted to hear the story behind it. "The closest associated story with Gemini is the legend of Castor and Polydeuces - Pollox in Latin - from Greek mythology. Castor and Polydeuces were identical twins born to Leda, Queen of Sparta, but they had two different fathers. It was said that Castor was the son of Leda's husband, King Tyndareus, who was mortal. Polydeuces was said to be the immortal son of Zeus, from Zeus's seduction of Leda while disguised as a swan. The same encounter also produced Helen of Troy. Tyndareus adopted Polydeuces. The twins were inseparable and became known as the Dioscuri."

"If I were to tell you more of the story, we'll be here much longer."

"You can tell me the rest another time."

"I can."

We stayed on the roof watching the stars fall and talking until Will's dad called us back inside.

We sat on the couch for a while. Just sitting. Not saying a thing. It felt good sitting in silence. It didn't feel wrong not talking.

Will's dad was already asleep. Will came from his

bedroom to sit for a while with me. He couldn't sleep either.

"Remember the time my dad said that I ran from the castle? Want to know what happened?"

I nodded, curious about where he was going with this.

"Something bad - like bad - happened, and for some reason, some of the boys training in my group thought it would be funny framing me."

I don't know who would think framing someone for something they didn't do would be funny. I know that people do this, but most of the time, the ones who do this are the ones who did the bad thing so that they'll never get caught.

"I was scared they actually believed them, so I ran away. I knew they told me not to. But it's what I felt to do."

He looked out the window at the dark outside. "It feels good doing things people tell you not to."

"I wouldn't know." I looked at him. "I have never done things people told me not to."

I was always used to do everything my mother told me, precisely as she said it. The same I did with Hecate. I never made something they told me not to.

I stared at the ceiling until my eyes hurt. Will's words stuck in my mind like honey to a spoon.

'It feels good doing things people tell you not to.'

I didn't know if it was true, and I wanted to know.

For sure, I wasn't thinking straight. I was tired. This wasn't something I would typically do.

I opened the window and went outside.

The meadow wasn't close enough to go there.

The silence of the night made me want to stay there for hours. But instead, the diffused sound of water running made me curious from where it came.

I jumped over the fence from the garden and went higher up the hill. My eyes didn't feel the need to see the village from up there.

From the top of the hill, I could see the river. It came from all over the woods, probably the same as in the meadow. It's water as clear as it should be.

I sat on my knees and stared at the water, seeing my reflection. I was the weirdest mix between my mother and my father. My mother had brown hair and caramel eyes. My father, well, I didn't know. The only times I remembered him, he didn't have that much appearance. My hair was red, and my eyes purple. Hard to understand how I got those. The only logical answer is that I got them from my father.

Chapter 9

It doesn't feel great having a dream after having a vision on the same day.

I was sitting at a table, staring at the sunset, in what seemed like a flower garden. From where I sat, I could see the sea. I felt like I was waiting for someone. But when I looked at the table, I only saw some books. When I looked in front of me, I saw a dark-skinned man wearing a black shirt and black pants, and boots. He had multiple dark rings, and only one of them was golden. His eyes were pitch black and hooded. He had a big nose and wide lips. His hair was as black as his eyes and braided in cornrows. He seemed young, maybe in his mid-twenties.

"I don't get it," I said, confused. "Why did she leave?"

"She didn't want to leave," the man said.

Then the dream changed.

I was sitting on a bench, looking at Will fighting a training puppet with a sword. He was wearing some light brown clothes.

"Maybe if you close your eyes, it'll be easier for it to

fight you," I teased him.

"Very funny, Flower," he said. "Very funny."

"Lili, come on! Let's go." I heard Will say from downstairs.

I ran down the stairs in the other dress I got from the attic. It was a baby blue mid-length dress. It had some thin straps and (my favorite part) pockets. Like actual fricking pockets. How cool is that?

I put my wand in my right boot and went out the door. Will had a backpack on his back where he put his stuff.

"You ready?"

"Nope," I told him.

He laughed. "Then we should get going. Dad's waiting a little further."

Today the town was peaceful. Only a few people were out. It was quite hot, after all. Roseberry waved us while going in the direction we came from. When we got to Will's dad, he informed me there was only about an hour until we reached the center.

We walked past a river and the place we were a few days ago. After we went to sleep, Will told me he would listen if I wanted to talk about what happened - or anything in general. The truth is I wanted to talk about it, but I was scared.

The trees were a brilliant color of green. Some of them even had flowers. The fields were full of poppies and wildflowers. From the flowers came a little rabbit. Nyx jumped off my shoulders and went to sniff the rabbit. I crouched next to it and started petting it.

"Hello, cutie," I said to the rabbit. He came closer and rubbed his head on my leg.

"Lili!" I heard Benjamin calling me.

"Just a second," I responded, returning to the rabbit. "If you go into the woods, you'll find not so far away a meadow with some carrots," I told the rabbit, and he started jumping into the woods.

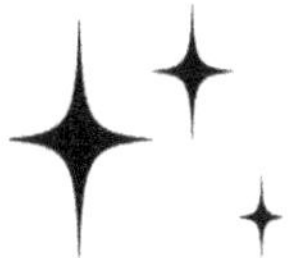

It was beautiful.

The base of the buildings was made out of brick, painted in multiple light and bright colors. Some of the buildings were covered in beautiful paneling. Almost under every window, there was a flower box. Most of the houses were one level, but the ones that had shops were two levels tall.

The streets had rock pavement that made a beautiful pattern that looked like flowers. It went right to the edge of the buildings, where some tables were out with chairs, and some people were sitting, drinking coffee. I could see people everywhere. They were all talking with each other, enjoying the beautiful day.

You could see the castle perfectly from the main street - the one we were on. It was made out of white marble. It had multiple towers with light blue roofs. As we got closer to it, it was even more gorgeous. The windows were big and decorated with black trim.

As we got further into the city, more stuff appeared. People were singing and dancing. Kids were sitting on the edge of the big fountain playing with the water.

All the streets led to where we were now sitting. This was the heart of the town, where all the festivals would take place. People of all ages were sitting on benches or tables, or walking, all having a good time.

The sound of happiness almost made me forget why we came here.

"You're drooling," Will laughed.

"Excuse me?" I tried to sound offended. He was right, after all. This place was so beautiful. I couldn't it compare with the village I used to live in.

Benjamin turned to us. "Before seeing the king, I have to do something. We'll meet here in about half an hour." He started walking on the street that we came from.

I looked around once more and pointed to a small shop with two tables by the window. "What's that?"

"That's the most famous bakery and candy shop in Lovskaria. Wanna go?" Will explain to me.

"I'd love to."

A sign fluttered in the wind above the door. On the sign, wrote *Patty's Treats.* The door was painted a light purple, which complimented the yellow paneling. I could see shelves full of bakery products and barrels full of sweets through the big window.

The bell on top of the door rang as we entered. The man at the counter waved at Will.

"Look all around. It has everything you could think about," Will told me.

The truth is that it had even more stuff than I could imagine.

First, it was sectioned into two parts: the bakery and the sweet shop. Second, it looked like it was taken out from one of the books my mother used to read me before sleep. The walls were bright yellow and painted with multiple small purple drawings. The shelves were made of oak, just like the other pieces of furniture (including the candy barrels). The floor was the same type of wood.

I looked at the bakery first. It had multiple bread types

and other patisserie products, like beagles.

Will put in the bag two croissants. I got lost in the smell of sweets and ended up on the candy side. It smelled like orange and freshly baked apple pie (a scent I could never forget) and grapes. A weird assortment of smells, but it smelled wonderful. The candy had small images on the walls, like a sheep, a pig, an apple, grapes, and many more. There were also some lollipops in multiple colors.

Will took a bag and put some blue ones with maybe blueberries in them.

"Anything you might like, Flower?"

"I think I'll stick with the croissant."

We went to the waiting line and, well, waited. Every few seconds people entered and went out of the shop. I looked at a picture on the wall. In it was a tall woman with short braided hair, a chunkier man, and three kids, two boys and one girl.

"Hello, Josh."

"Hello, Will and..."

"Lili. Nice to meet you, sir."

He seemed to be around fifty, with "salt and pepper" hair and sweet brown eyes.

"Nice to meet you. Did you know that new customers don't have to pay for the first purchase?"

"I did not," I told him. "But I'm not the one paying. I don't have any money."

"Then Will won't have to pay."

"Josh, it's not necessary."

"You know the drill, Will. New customers, no paying," insisted Josh.

"How's Patty doing?" asked Will, trying to change the subject.

"You ain't fooling me, young man. But to answer your question, Patty is better than ever. She's in the back making some lollipops."

"Nice to hear." Will put some silver coins on the table. "See you next time!"

"It was nice to meet you, Lili."

As we went out of the shop, John exclaimed. "Wait, Will! You didn't have to."

I giggled. "You are a nice person, Sapphires."

We sat on the edge of the fountain, next to the children playing with the water. I sat with my legs crossed. Will gave me my croissant, and I took a bite. It tasted like a warm summer day filled with melted butter and the softest chocolate ever.

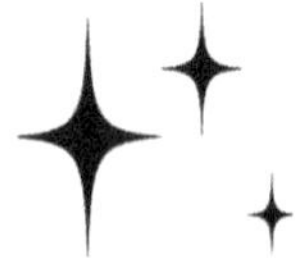

I was just a few meters from entering the castle area and was scared.

The gates of the castles were open, revealing three beautiful arches. As I stepped into the area, I could see people looking at me. Sometimes my red hair brings more eyes on me than if I would scream. It's even worse if they question my purple eyes.

On the stairs we were walking on, a girl with a blue dress stood at the end of them, looking bored. Behind her, a girl in a much less fancy dress yelled at some guards. I couldn't make out what she said.

"Princess Elizabeth." Will and Benjamin bowed at the royal, so I did the same.

"Benjamin, Will, a pleasure as always," she said excitedly. "And I suppose you are Lili."

Her blue eyes were full of sadness and stress. But, strangely, her energy was shining with happiness and pressure. The only thing that could hide her pain was her diamond smile.

"A pleasure to meet you, your majesty," I said, questioning where she knew my name. She probably heard it from the letters Benjamin sent to the king.

"You can call me Elizabeth or Liz." She took a pause to think. "Or even Lizzie. Anything but 'your majesty.' I'm not that old. "

"All right, Elizabeth," I said, smiling at her.

Benjamin looked at me with a dead stare.

"Liz, come and look!" the girl behind her called her.

"I'll see you around; I guess," the princess said, turning back to the girl.

Benjamin started walking in front of us. We were walking through a big, wide corridor with tall pillars, the color of the sea I saw in my mother's paintings. In person, I've never seen the sea up close. I always wanted, but my mother said it was too dangerous for us to travel that far.

"You are brave to call the princess by her name," Will whispered.

"If she wants to be called by her name, that's what I'll call her by," I told him. "She is royalty. Her words are my command."

"You know how to play with rules."

"Of course I do," I smirked, and we laughed silently. But, of course, he didn't know about my 'escape,' and how I broke the rules his father set for me, so we didn't laugh for the same reason.

We stopped in front of some oversized blue doors with

silver handles.

"Once we go inside," Benjamin told us, "you'll let me talk."

"But you don't know how Will found me."

"And when the king asks something, you will answer *politely*," he said, ignoring me.

The big doors opened, letting out an old man.

"Next!" yelled a man from inside.

The throne room was as big as two houses, one next to the other. The walls were painted white. All the room's windows - floor to ceiling - had the same ocean-blue curtains.

Four thrones sat in front of a window on the other side of the room. The giant throne had a man sitting on it. The other three thrones were empty.

The matching color carpet felt like a cloud when I walked on it.

When the king saw us, he gestured to the servant next to him to get everyone out. In seconds, Will, Benjamin, the king and I were the only ones in the room.

"Ben, my friend, I see you finally came," exclaimed the king.

"Your majesty," said Benjamin while Will and I bowed

at the king.

"Will, I've been informed that you'll stay here for a few weeks for training."

"That's right, your majesty," Will agreed.

The king turned his eyes to Benjamin. "Now, let's discuss why you came here."

I started to get tense.

The king played a little with his brown beard, thinking. He was dressed in a deep blue robe, his golden crown shining.

"I see you found a witch," he said, and I felt like my breath was cut. I tried controlling my heartbeat.

"Yes, sir. And..." Benjamin started saying, just to be cut by Will.

"I found her in the woods, sir. Unfortunately, she was attacked by a pack of wolves."

"Will," his dad said sharply.

"I would like to know the witch's name. Will you tell it to me, girl?" the king said, addressing me.

"My name is Lilium Grace," I said, shaking. I could feel the heat in the tips of my fingers. The same way I felt the day before.

Please, not now, I prayed.

Will grabbed my hand, probably seeing my fingertips turn purple. When he touched my hand, it felt like a shock was sent to my heart.

Benjamin started telling the king his side of the story. Many of the things he said weren't right, but I wouldn't argue with him in front of the king.

"You okay?" Will whispered to me.

"Holding up for now," I told him with a small fake smile. He just held my hand tighter.

"I'd like to hear Will's side of the story and then Lilium's." I like how he didn't refer to me as *the witch*. This way, I felt more welcomed.

Will told the king what actually happened. When he talked about the cut he got on his leg, his dad turned toward us, surprised. He didn't speak about what happened a few days ago, which made me feel better.

When it was my time, I just added some story points, like The Smokes and the Meadow.

"I understand," the king said, looking at Will and me. "Let me think for a moment."

"Shall we go out, your majesty?" Benjamin asked. For some reason, the question sounded like he was asking the king to go out on a date.

"No, no. You can stay."

A minute passed, and then another. The heat in my hands grew hotter, and I grabbed Will's hand tighter.

"I've made my mind," announced the king.

Beads of sweat started running down my forehead. The time seemed to go slower, and my heart beat faster.

Then the king spoke. "I don't see any bad thing you did, Lilium. You don't seem like a bad witch. Powerful, yes, but bad, no."

A rock was lifted from my heart.

"You are allowed to go wherever you want in Lovskaria, and no one will know you are a witch. You are from now on under the protection of the Lovskaria Kingdom."

"Thank you, your majesty," I said, not even trying to hide my happiness.

Will's dad remained to discuss the village's needs with the king. Then, the servants started going back into the room.

"Thank you," I told Will, hugging him as tight as possible.

"You don't have to thank me for anything."

"I actually do. Without you, I would probably be in a cell by now."

"Well, now you are part of this kingdom."

I looked through the big window at the kingdom below

us. People were out on the streets doing their daily work, living the best life.

"It seems like I am," I told him softly.

I wonder how many witches are under the protection of the king. And the fact that he knows how powerful I am is weird. What does he know that I don't?

Chapter 10

I think you know what I'm going to say.

Since the king gave me his protection, my life's been going up. No one knows I'm a witch and no one will. I can go where ever I want and do what I want. As long as I am under the king's protection, no creature hunter can hurt me. (At least, I hope.)

After the visit to the castle, I went straight to the meadow. To be honest, the meadow took good care of itself. I even found the rabbit I met on the way to the city - and named it Sunny.

Today is the first day I have gone to visit Will since he started training. Also the second time I'm going to the city.

I changed into a pine green skirt, a white shirt, and a brown corset.

Nyx was lying on the bed. I sat next to him.

"Do you want to come with me, kitty?" I asked him, patting his head. He just seemed to get sleepier.

"Meow."

I walked to the door, and I picked up a white headscarf from the table.

I stood at the door, waiting for Nyx to come with me. Instead, he just made himself cozier on my bed. I started walking down the hill, putting the headscarf on my head.

The woods in the daytime are a lovely place. No evil spirits, no smoke, just friendly animals that don't want to hurt you.

The birds are singing as always. Some squirrels jump from tree to tree. I picked up some rocks and sticks and put them in my satchel.

When I returned from the castle, I found a shortcut and had arrived at least fifteen minutes earlier than usually.

I walked on the road holding one hand on the bag handle. The sky was clear, and the sun was shining as bright as always.

As I got closer to the city, the sound of life got louder and louder. Being used to not hearing this much sound, I can't imagine how people can live around this much noise. I could hear multiple songs coming from numerous directions. The smell of freshly baked goods could lead me to every bakery and shop. But I promised Will I'll meet him today. We kept in touch through letters, with the help of one of my bird friends. (One of the perks of feeding animals for free.)

Once I got to the fountain, I asked a middle age man where the entrance to the castle training grounds was. I took left from the road leading to the main entrance. In just a few minutes, I stood in front of an open gate. While walking to the gate, I could see some people taking a glance at me - mostly kids, and I didn't mind that.

At the entrance, a tall guard dressed in the Kingdom's color pallete asked me what I wanted.

"I'm here to see one of the guards in training."

He looked at me from head to toe. "Walk to the right, and you'll see a wooden door. Open it, and you'll get in the training grounds."

"Thank you."

I walked in the direction the guard told me to. When I opened the door, I saw a bunch of teenagers with swords fighting each other. Next to them were some guards, giving them instructions. I counted about twenty boys and two girls, but there were probably more.

I looked around round for Will. He was at the other end of the garden, training with a dark-haired boy; I couldn't determine if he had brown or black hair. The guard was correcting some of their moves.

Will spotted me and stopped. Unfortunately, his opponent took advantage of that and knocked him over.

"Attention, Miller!" the guard told him.

I giggled, walked to a bench, sat in front of it, and waited for them to finish. Finally, Will said something to the guard and walked to a door that led to the castle. On his way to the door, he showed me his hand, with all his fingers up, indicating that he'll come in five minutes.

The boy that Will trained with came next to me.

"Sebastian," he introduced himself.

"Seb, then," I told him. "I'm Lili."

He looked around sixteen. His hair was dark brown, just like his eyes. His hair was cut short on the sides, and his front one pushed back. He was taller than Will, but not by much.

"Where did you meet Will?" he asked me.

He was hard to read, so I didn't know if I could trust him, but I decided to tell the truth. "We met somewhere near his village."

I meant half of the truth.

"It's good to see him make more friends," he said with a smile. "Not to brag, but I *was* Will's only friend."

"How did *you* meet Will," I asked him.

"I know him since we were about eight - he was eight, I was nine. He used to come here almost every week because his mother was still a guard. At one point, Lizzy wanted me to meet him."

"You mean the princess?"

"Yep. Anyway, she wanted me to meet him because she read some of the guards' papers and saw that I would train with Will."

"She seems like a nice person."

"Nicer than you think... So is Will."

"He is the nicest person I've ever met," I smiled.

I saw Will coming our way. He had changed into a greenish shirt and some black pants.

"I'll get going. Lizzy is waiting for me," Seb told me and went in the direction Will was coming from. He patted Will on the back, which made me laugh.

"Hi," I told him.

"Hi," he said. "I see you met Seb."

"He seemed nice."

"Shall we go? Not that I don't want to stay here, but I think if Capitan would see me still here, he'll put me train again," he laughed.

We walked past the guard at the entrance. He said hello to Will and asked him where he was going. Will told me that we were going to Patty's.

The guard wasn't probably that fast with thinking. If he was, he would've realized that Patty's opened today at one, and now it was eleven.

When we were out of the guard's sight, I asked Will, "We're not going to Patty's, are we?"

"Nope. I wanted to show you something I found the other day. I didn't understand, but I thought you might know it."

"You told me to come just for this?" I said, trying to sound disappointed.

"Of course not, Flower." He didn't think this through. "We're going to go to the center after."

We got to the center, and I looked around. Will started walking to the right; from this direction, kids were coming. The street was even more colorful. I saw strings going from balcony to balcony with clothes drying on them. Paper airplanes were flying from house to house. Kids were playing with a ball on the street and started playing tag with them again.

One girl ran into me and said that she was sorry.

"Don't worry, dear," I told her. Her hair was brighter than mine, and her eyes the color of a cornflower. She went back to her friends and started playing with them tag again. I had the feeling that I'll see that girl again.

I caught back with Will, who was waiting for me at the

end of the street.

"Is that the sea?" I asked Will, looking at the water in front of us.

"Yes. But it looks better from the taller hills or castle gardens."

"How long till we get to what you wanted to show me?"

"A few minutes."

"Are you going to tell me what you found?"

"I think it's better that you see with your own eyes. I don't know what they are."

We walked along the sealine. Its water was as clear as a rock crystal quart. Some fish were swimming a little further away in the water. I could see some seaweed and other plants on the bottom.

A little further away, the forest was starting. We walked towards the city until we came to its entrance.

"Wouldn't it have been easier if we had walked through the city to here?" I asked him.

"The city is bustling at this hour."

I walked faster so I was at Will's side. "How's the training going?"

"Better than any time," I could tell he was lying just from his voice.

I decided to push my luck. "Things aren't going great, are they?"

"It's just... Gosh! I don't know. I love what I'm doing. This is what I want to do for a living."

"Then what's wrong?" I asked him.

"Dad told our trainer to be more severe, and to every little thing I do wrong, repeat and repeat and repeat until I make it perfectly. I know he wants the best for me, but... I just need a break."

He looked to the side and stopped walking.

"We're here," he announced.

He was looking at an old tree trunk a little outside the woods. Something sparkled inside of it. I went in front of Will and looked inside the tree trunk.

Inside it, there were a bunch of weird spheres. They were all different shades of purple. They all shone so brightly that I had to blink a few times to see them better.

"What are they?" I murmured.

"I don't know. That's why I wanted you to come and see," he told me from behind my shoulder. "I figured out that they were something related to magic."

I took one of the objects and analyzed it. It looked like a huge bead made out of marble. It was really heavy also and about the size of my hand.

The other object was the same shape but cut in half.

I took some old pieces of material kept in my satchel and put the entire thing in one and one of the sliced ones in the other piece of fabric I had.

"We should cover them with something so nobody finds them," I told Will.

He looked around and took a piece of wood from the ground that probably came from the tree the objects were in. He put it over the things without squishing them and backed away.

"Let's go to Patty's," Will said.

As we got further away from the tree trunk, I started hearing hundreds of voices. I looked back, and the sound disappeared.

"Did you hear that?"

"Hear what?"

"Nothing," I said, thinking I only imagined the sounds.

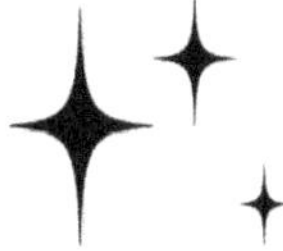

I was meditating under the willow tree in the meadow. Hecate was sitting somewhere near me. I was peeking with one of my eyes to see where she was sitting.

"Stop trying to see where I am," she said like she

was reading my mind - which she was probably doing. "Concentrate on your spell."

"But I don't get what this spell is for," I said, opening my eyes and looking at her. Just like last time, she was dressed in a black dress. This time she wasn't wearing her tiara.

"It's a protection spell that will make it harder for Eris to go into your mind. I don't think you want to know what would have happened if you had lost control that day."

"That's because you didn't tell me the spell could make me lose control."

"You didn't lose control because of the spell; you lost control because of your emotions."

She came in front of me and sat cross-legged.

"You've been bottling up all of your emotions for years. Then, one powerful emotion and the bottle got a crack. At one point, the bottle will break, and everything you've been keeping inside will spill everywhere. You know very well that emotions control magic. Emotions are one of the most powerful things in the world. You have to control them."

"And what if they control me?" I asked softly.

From somewhere in the back, Nyx came and sat in my lap.

Hecate bit her lip softly. "I don't have an answer for that, but you'll learn to control them in time. You just have to have hope in yourself and the right people around you."

"You mean Will, don't you?"

"I don't know. If you want, ask Aphrodite."

"Aphrodite played with my life?" I shouted.

"I wasn't supposed to tell you that." She laughed softly. "But I can tell you this: it will be hard for you two in the future."

"Thanks. That's very encouraging," I said sarcastically. Hecate just smiled.

I looked for a second behind me. I could see what I had found earlier that day from my satchel. I took another one of the green things out of the bag. I gave Hecate the broken one.

"Do you know what these are?"

She looked stunned at them. She turned the broken pieces on all sides, looking at every inch.

"I have no idea what those are, but I will take this with me to Mount Olympus and ask the other gods. They might know what this is. One thing about them is clear."

"What?"

"They're burning my hands," she put the half spheres on the ground.

"They didn't burn mine," I told her.

"Things act differently to different persons."

She got up and gave me her hand so I would get up.

"I think it's time for me to go. And one thing: I think telling your friend about the other gods, and I, is a good idea. I don't think you want him to go crazy if he finds out on his own."

"I sure don't want that," I said as she turned in a pile of glitter, and then the realization came in. "Aphrodite played with my life?"

 Chapter 11

The things that haunt her in the middle of the night are the things that will destroy everything.

In the castle, the silence was supreme. The only person walking the halls was Princess Elizabeth. She was headed towards the throne room.

She didn't enter the room because she heard her father speak. The door wasn't fully shut, so she looked through the small opening and listened.

"Your majesty, she killed all those innocent people. How could you let her live?" asked the butler.

"Because that wasn't her," the king responded.

"But, your majesty, she's a witch! She could hurt our people."

"My people, Greg!" the king said, tired of the discussion.

From the crack between the doors, the princess could see the king sitting on his throne, in his ocean blue robes and golden crown slightly tilted on the side of his head, and Greg the butler standing next to the throne.

"What if she hurts them? What if she is actually evil?"

"Are you not trusting my decisions, Greg?" the king barked at the butler.

"No, my lord."

"Then?"

The princess pushed the door end entered the throne room. She put on a fake smile - the one she always uses - and walked to the throne podium.

Her dress was covering her shoes, so her father couldn't see she was wearing black boots and not the shoes her mother gave her. That's the way she was. She loved breaking the rules as long as nobody knew. Wearing combat boots at a royal banquet? She did that way to many times. Dated before sixteen? She's done that. Not letting guards accompany her on her daily walks through the city? Every day. She's done more than every princess in every kingdom.

"You're free, Greg," the king said.

The princess didn't talk until the butler closed the door. She didn't like him very much.

"Father."

"Elizabeth."

"I've come to tell you that Mother's looking for you. She asks for your opinion on some of the decorations for my birthday."

He looked sweet at his daughter. "My dear, but why aren't you choosing the decorations."

"I chose the decorations, but she wants your opinion on some other decoration she refuses to tell me about."

"Oh, yes. I'll go and see her now."

He rose from his throne and went past his daughter.

While her parents were occupied, the princess enjoyed her free time and went to the training grounds. That's one of the things she loves the most.

She changed into high-waist brown pants and a simple long-sleeved button shirt that she tucked in her pants and put her honey-blonde hair in a high ponytail. Her boots were the same as the ones she had worn earlier, but brown.

The training grounds were empty at that time of the day.

Next to the swords, Sebastian was waiting for his girlfriend to come. He threw her sword at her, and she caught it perfectly.

"You're getting better at this," the boy said.

Elizabeth smiled. "If I'm getting attacked, I'm not going to wait for a guard to save me. I'd rather save myself."

"And what if that guard is me?" Sebastian smirked, coming closer to the princess.

"Then, I might allow you to save me." She said, getting on her tippy toes and kissing her boyfriend. "But until then, I'll learn to defend myself."

She raised her sword, and they started fighting. The blades made a clang every time they hit each other.

"You're not keeping your legs shoulder width apart, and you should step forward as if you were to shake my hand, Lizzie."

Elizabeth did just as he told her.

"See, don't you think that's better?" he asked her. "Now, try to hit me."

She nodded. The princess gripped the sword with both hands and raised it above her head. She launched herself toward Sebastian, bringing the sword down with all her might and power. She didn't even see Sebastian move out of her way. Her legs were swept out from under her, forcing her upper body onto the grass. Before she could collect herself, a firm strike of the pommel of Sebastian's sword knocked the breath out of her lungs, along with any trace of dignity.

The boy helped his girlfriend get off the ground. "Confidence may push you forward, but hubris will get you killed," he said.

The princess rolled her eyes.

"Don't roll your eyes at me like that, Liz! You know you would've been killed if you had done this in a battle."

"I was just so close to winning!" the princess pouted.

"I know, Lizzie, but you didn't pay enough attention to me."

"That sounded awfully selfish," she laughed.

"I know" the boy smiled. "Lesson three: keep your strikes deliberate and disciplined. Do not give your enemy any opportunity for retribution. And what did I say about your feet?"

Elizabeth resumed her stance and followed Sebastian's instructions as she always did. They danced that way for hours until the sun hung low in the purple and pink sky. Parries became more calculated and footwork more thoughtful. She did not land a single strike on him but felt a couple of centimeters more comfortable with the sword; after all, this was just her fifth lesson.

They stopped when the sun was completely down, and the sky was full of stars.

Elizabeth let herself fall on the grass and relax. She was breathing hard because of the training.

"I'm going to need a bath after this," she said. "A big, bubbly, long bath."

Sebastian sat next to her.

"How are you so not tired?" she asked.

"I've been training for eight years. Trust me; you forget what pain is after the first year."

Elizabeth looked at him like he was kidding, but his face said otherwise.

Eight years is a long time. They have known each other since they were babies. Sebastian's dad became head guard after the old head guard - Nyota - died in battle almost five years ago. Ever since, Sebastian's dad has been all over the top, making sure that when he dies, Sebastian will be able to take on the lead of being a Head guard. The two barely had any time to hang out anymore. Elizabeth had even more princess duties, and Sebastian had even more training. They don't think twice about it every time they have a chance to be together.

The princess put her head on her boyfriend's chest and looked at the sky. Then, he started playing with her blonde hair.

They stayed on the grass for just ten more minutes until the princess was called by her maid, Aideen. Elizabeth rose, said good night to Sebastian, and went to her room with her friend.

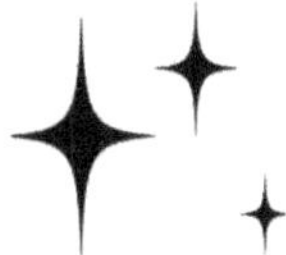

She couldn't sleep.

Every time she closed her eyes, she saw the thing that haunted her dreams.

She sat on her bed, trying not to fall asleep. She got up and went to her desk. She walked on the fuzzy rug that covered the middle of the room, leaving behind the canopy bed.

She unlocked the desk drawer, took out her journal, and sat on the chair. From the drawer, she took a pencil and opened the journal to the last used page. Sleepless nights led to her filling the pages of the journal with drawings of the thing that haunted her dreams.

The thing had a woman's body, almost washed out of colors. Her eyes were milky white, so piercing that it seemed she was staring straight through your soul. Her hair was so thin and dark that it looked like string. Her lips were as dried as a desert. She wore a tall dress that made her look like a ghost.

There wasn't a night Elizabeth didn't see the woman in her dreams. Most of the nights she spends at her desk, obsessively drawing her nightmare. Every time she closed her eyes, she would see her.

A powerful wind blew through the open balcony door. The princess walked to close the door.

"Hello," said an unknown voice.

Elizabeth froze. She opened her eyes slowly, her breathing getting faster and faster.

When she saw the woman of her nightmares, she slammed the door closed and ran to hide on the other side of her bed, far from the balcony.

She hugged her knees and tried not to cry out of fear.

"You can run, but you can't hide," said the woman in front of her.

She tried moving, but she was stuck to the ground. She screamed, but no one could hear her. It was like her lips were glued together. She closed her eyes crying, but when she opened them up, she was in her bed, and the sun was shining through the curtains of her floor-to-ceiling windows.

The princess looked at her nightstand and saw her journal with a name written repeatedly on the page: Eris.

Chapter 12

I put the plates down on the tables. I said "Enjoy" to the people that sat at the table. They gave me back smiles and started eating.

From the back of the counter, Ivy called me.

She was a year older than me. Her skin was the color of coffee, with lighter patches on her skin - vitiligo - one right on the inner corner of the right eye, one on her chin, and a little on the lip. She had lighter patches of skin on her arms too. Her hair was braided in long dark brown braids that matched her eyes. Her dress was a bright yellow.

She had the attention span of a five-year-old child and the heart of one. Ivy's mother didn't know that she was working at the pub. *No Ivy would be left if her mother knew - as Ivy described it.*

"I'll have to leave soon," she told me. "Do you think you can handle this alone?"

I looked around the room. Around thirty people sat at the table, and three guys were at the bar.

"I think I will."

"In about an hour, this place should be empty." She put on her shoulder a white towel. "It always is. No one comes here at that hour."

"It's good. I'll have time to eat, and you'll have time to return." I turned so I wouldn't be facing the people.

"Are you sure you can handle this alone?"

"Yeah, of course."

"Thank you so much! I'll be back as soon as possible!"

She left the towel on the counter and ran out of the front door. Some people looked at her. Unlike me, she wasn't the kind of girl to care about what other people thought of her. Ivy was the kind of person witches called a free spirit.

From the kitchen, Miss Miliani called me. I took the plates of food from her and delivered them to the person that ordered them.

I went to the new customers that sat by the window. One of them I recognized was Sebastian. One of the other two had buzz-cut brown hair, and the other had long blond hair.

"What would it be, boys?" I said, taking out my little notepad and pencil.

Sebastian looked up at me. "Lili, hi!" He looked stunned to see me. But, of course, if I saw myself working in a pub, I would be stunned too. "Guys, this is Lili. Lili, these are Evander and Dean."

Dean was the one with the buzz cut, and Evander was the one with the long blond hair.

"We'll get three steaks with whatever toppings Miss Miliani chooses," said Evander.

"You are really following in Ivy's footsteps," said Sebastian. "She started working here when she was eleven."

I was shocked when Miss Miliani said I could work at the pub. I didn't understand why she would hire someone under sixteen to work here.

"Tell Will I say Hi." I smiled and walked to the kitchen. I told Miss Miliani what the three boys wanted.

"I'll make them as soon as possible," she said sweetly.

If I understood correctly from what Ivy told me, Miss Miliani didn't always own the pub. Her sister created it and managed it. After her death, Miss Miliani didn't want to see her sister's dream die with her, so she started managing it and working in the kitchen.

"Lili?" she asked. "Could you stay longer tonight? I need to go buy some things for tomorrow."

"Of course."

Miss Miliani said I didn't need to deal with the guys that sat at the bar. She said she'd care for them, but that didn't mean I wasn't supposed to clean the bar.

The pub was empty. It was only me cleaning the front, and Miss Miliani was in the back, counting the money we had made so far today.

I heard the door open and thought that Ivy had come back.

"Interesting job for a fourteen-year-old girl," said the familiar voice of Will.

"Will," I turned to him with a smile. "What can I get you?"

"Nothing. I'm not hungry."

I pointed to the sign above the bar that said *"No buying? No staying."*

"I know you don't want to, but Miss Miliani does. How about some apple pie?"

"Apple pie will do." He smiled.

I turned around and took a plate. In it, I placed a piece of apple pie.

"How did you start working here?" he asked.

"Last week, when we were here, I heard Ivy discussing this job. So I talked a little with the place's owner, and now you don't have to pay for the things I want to buy."

"I didn't mind that!" he tried sounding offended.

"Well, I did. Plus, if people see me more, they'll suspect

less."

"If you say so."

He was surrounded by playful ness, almost like Ivy, but he wasn't usually like this.

I looked up at Will and saw that his shoulders had started relaxing. His sapphire blue eyes turned lighter and happier.

"What happened?" I asked him.

"Nothing."

"Sapphs, you are literally radiating happiness."

"I don't know. I had a pretty good week. So maybe that's why." He smiled.

"Your happiness seems bigger than a good week."

"Maybe because I'm seeing you."

I blushed lightly. "Don't be silly! You'll see me all the time now!"

"That's why!"

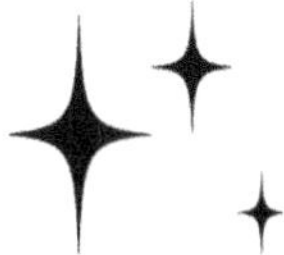

Miss Miliani left a couple of minutes after I finished cleaning the tables.

I went down the hallway to the files room. I unlocked the door and started looking through the room. It was small, around the same size as the living room in my old house. The walls were painted a dirty beige.

Behind the wooden table, I saw the drawers made out of the same wood. Every drawer had stickers with different letters and numbers, probably for every year or so. I tried opening one, but the wooden drawers barely opened. So I decided not to force them anymore.

I looked at the desk. It was full of files and papers and pens. The files were placed on the table, from the oldest to the most recent. I saw that one of them had written *"death"*.

I pulled the chair and sat on it. I put my legs up on the desk.

I opened the file; her name was on the first page - Galen Miliani. I looked at the following pages and read some of the things written on them. I learned that she was forty-nine at the time of her death. She had no children. Her husband died two years ago from the same illness she died from.

In between the pages, I found a note. Something was written in beautiful cursive letters, but I couldn't understand what it said.

The ink was as black as a raven and washed out.

Some of the things she did and stuff about the pub were

written on the next couple of pages. Just as Ivy said, Miss Miliani took the pub because she didn't want her sister's dream to die, but also - probably - from the fact that in Galen's will was written to whom she would wish the pub to go to.

I heard the front door open and rushed to close the file. I put some things over the file, trying to cover it, so it would look the same as when I found it. I put my legs down near the table.

I expected to see Miss Miliani entering the room. Instead, I saw a girl with a long flowery cape with a hood attached. She looked quite young, maybe fifteen or sixteen.

"I'm guessing that you are Lili," the girl said with a strong British accent, removing her hood. She had gorgeous blonde hair and blue eyes. Her face was the definition of perfect. Her button nose shone in the dim light of the room, and her lips were the color of the prettiest light pink I'd ever seen. She was dressed in a soft blue turtle neck shirt, brown pants, and brown boots.

"Are you Lili?" she asked again.

"Yes," I said, not knowing what she was doing there.

She came closer, resting her hands on the desk, making her golden neckless move like a clock pendulum.

"I need your help," she said.

Only then did I realize who she was.

The princess had sad blue eyes and happy energy. She was hiding her true self and her pain behind a mask.

"I'll help you," I said.

"You'll help me?" she said, relaxing her shoulders.

"Of course."

"But you don't even know who I am."

"Princess," I said, putting one leg over the other. "I don't have that short of memory. I could recognize you just by the energy you give. Now, with what can I help you?"

"Listen, I know that you are a witch."

"Your father told you?"

"No, he did not." She looked straight into my eyes. "I realize that on my own."

"How?"

"My father only asks for an 'alone' conversation when he talks with a witch, and I heard him talking the other day about a witch. So I put two and two together and realized he was talking about you."

"What was he talking about and with whom?" I said, feeling my hands heat up. I moved uncomfortably on my chair. I didn't know whether to trust her or not. I could feel she wasn't a bad person, but I wasn't sure I could trust her.

"That's... none of your business."

"It's very well my business," I said, accidentally knocking some things off the desk, leaving them free to the eye. I hurried and tried to cover it with some other papers on the desk, but Elizabeth took the file before I could cover it.

I heard the front door open. Elizabeth turned and looked at me, asking what should we do.

I shoved Galen's file under the desk and whispered to Elizabeth, "I know a spell that might help us. Just sit in the corner and be careful not to say something."

I took the wand out of my boot and pointed to the princess. I imagined that she was invisible. I closed my eyes, and when I opened them back, I couldn't see the princess. Either the spell worked, or Elizabeth jumped out the window.

Miss Miliani came into the room looking tired. She left on the drawers some bags that seemed to have some vegetables and other stuff in them.

"Thank you so much for staying late today, Lili. You saved me!" she said, pushing her green glasses on her nose.

"Any time, Miss Miliani."

I looked at the window and saw that the curtains were moving. The spell worked. I made some subtle hand signs telling Elizabeth to stop moving.

Miss Miliani looked at the floor. She picked up off the floor the things I pushed off the desk, including the file.

"When the door opened, I startled and accidentally pushed those off the desk," I lied.

"It's no problem, dear."

I took my satchel and rose off the chair. My white cardigan almost got caught in the chair. I arranged my skirt and walked to the door of the office.

While the woman was still down, I signed Elizabeth out of the room. I felt how she walked by me and went into the hallway.

"Good night, Miss Miliani!"

"Do you live close to here? It's quite dark outside. I don't want you walking alone at this hour."

I thought it was sweet of her to think about my safety, but I had to lie. She couldn't know that I was living in an old cabin in the middle of the woods. If she knew, she would've done everything so I would live somewhere in the city.

"I live close," I lied, smiling at her.

"Good night, dear."

"Good night."

I turned and walked the hallway. When I opened the

door, I waited to feel Elizabeth's presence exit, and then I went out the door too.

I took the wand out of my boot and imagined that Elizabeth was visible again. Then, when I opened my eyes, I could see Elizabeth again.

"That was one of the coolest things I have ever done!" she said.

"I used to make myself invisible when I was little and scare Mom. Then, after every time I'd scared her that way, we would laugh together about it."

Whenever mom returned from her job late at night, I hid behind the door or the couch and scared her. I started doing this from the first day I learned the spell - I was maybe five - until the day she died. Only now did I realize that she always knew I was hiding, but she always played scared, even if she wasn't.

That whole thought made my eyes teary.

I washed away that thought and turned to the princess.

"I don't think it's a great idea to talk here on the street," she said.

"Does your dad know you are here?" I asked her.

"No, he doesn't."

"How long will it take him to realize?"

"Probably another hour and a half or two. But my mother will realize quicker, in - let's say - an hour."

"Let's go to my house."

"How much will we make until there?"

"Just a few seconds."

She looked at me like I was a mad woman. "A few seconds?"

"You'll see," I smiled foxily. "Take my hand."

I took my wand and spun it around our heads.

"Let's hope we don't end up in front of your parents."

I thought about my cabin. I imagined sitting in front of the fireplace with the princess next to me.

An white fume started swirling around our feet, working its way up to our heads.

Elizabeth looked fascinated at my magic, turning her head to see every bit of it.

She tried putting her hand through it, but I hit her hand, stopping it. If she had put her hand through it, the spell would've broken, and we would still be in the middle of the street in Lovskaria.

The only thing we could see for a few seconds was the white fume, which started disappearing from the top, swirling around us.

I could see my washed-out brick fireplace.

When the fume completely dissolved, I sat on the couch and removed my boots. It felt so good getting them off after wearing them for a full day. The soft, fuzzy rug touched my tired legs.

"Well, we didn't end up before your parents."

I went to the table and invited Elizabeth to sit at it.

I took two green mugs from the cupboard and put some water in them. Then, I took them in my hands and sat them on the table, one in front of the princess and one in front of where I sat.

"How did you do that?" she asked, still looking at the place we arrived, amazed.

"Magic. I'm a witch. Not all witches do evil spells. I don't think that there are any more witches with poison apples to give to pretty princesses to take the throne. So no need to worry, princess," I said jokingly.

Elizabeth looked at me with her head tilted to the side and giving a little laugh. Her face changed emotions really fast. She now looked at me seriously.

"I think you are the only person who can help me. I've had the same kind of dream for the past few months."

I didn't interrupt her. I let her finish what she had to say.

"Every time the dream starts out normal - sunshine,

flowers, ponies, nice stuff - but when the dream is at the end or at the nicest moment," she paused, trying to find her words. "This-this thing that has the body of a woman with white eyes that stare into my soul, and her hair is like string. Her lips are as dried as a desert. She is dressed in a tool dress that makes her look like a ghost. Every morning I wake up screaming from dreaming and sweaty, and I barely sleep at night! I don't even remember when I last slept an entire night! And yesterday morning, I woke up with my notebook with a name written obsessively on the page. I don't remember writing 'Eris' in the middle of the night."

I felt like someone threw a pie in my face. If she was actually talking about Eris, things were horrible.

"I got the notebook with me." She took a white notebook out of her cape. She opened it to a page that wrote '14th of May'.

The drawings were made with a purplish pencil, one next to the other. Liz turned pages until the entire notebook was full. As she said, 'Eris' was written obsessively on the last page. The drawings were just as she described them. And more importantly, the drawings were of Eris.

I wanted to crawl into a ball and roll around the room. I wanted to cry. I wanted to scream at the gods for making my life like this.

I looked at my fingers, and I saw the tip of them turn purple. This time I had no Will to help me. I clenched my fist, my nails digging into my skin.

"What did she say?" I asked, somewhere between trying not to cry and trying not to scream.

"She said that I can run, but I can't hide. In other dreams, she says that I'll meet her and that she will always haunt me, and a lot of other stuff." I could hear in her voice how scared she was.

"That's the way Eris is. She doesn't stop until she gets what she wants. I want to say that she'll stop, but the truth is that she won't. She never does!" I said with all the emotions I'd been holding in.

"How do you know?" she looked at me with sadness.

"She's been haunting me ever since I was a baby! She never let me live in peace! She sent people to kill my mother and me! That's how I know, Elizabeth! That's how I know!" I screamed and uncapped my emotions. "That's how I know..."

A cold and slow river started flowing down my cheeks. I wiped the tears away.

"I can't help you get rid of her, but I can help you learn why she appears in your dreams. I would do anything to help you know what she wants from you."

"She killed your mother?" she asked, looking at me with her head tilted to the side, her voice little.

"She did many things to me, yes, being one of them, but she won't do that to you and your family. I won't let her do that."

"On my birthday - fourteenth of June - there's going to be a festival and a ball, where castle's doors will be open so the guests can enter. We'll meet in a safe place. Is that fine with you?"

"Yes," I responded. "Now I think it's time for you to go back. I can 'teleport' us to the training grounds because I've been there, but you'll have to return to your room alone. Shall I start the spell?"

The princess nodded, and I went next to her and touched her shoulder. Then, with my wand, I circled our heads, and the orange fume started appearing from the ground.

When it disappeared, we were on the training grounds all alone. I told Elizabeth goodnight, and she went inside the castle.

I looked around once more, used the spell, and returned to my cabin.

Eris really wants to make me give up and let her take control. She was like a crack in a wall; with time, it gets bigger and bigger, and once it's big enough, everything falls. That's what she wants.

Elizabeth's plan was perfect, except for one thing.

On the fourteen of June, it was my birthday too.

Chapter 13

I love cookies.

I sat crouched behind the old beige sofa in the living room. I could see my mother open the door. She was the most beautiful woman I had ever seen in my life. She was tall, confident, smart and sweet. Her face was so beautiful; Aphrodite would be jealous. Her caramel eyes were full of hope and life. Her long and wavy milk chocolate hair was untied and free, falling on her back like a shiny river. She was quite young, only twenty-six. My grandma always said that I ruined my mother's life and that if my father didn't appear in her life, she would've been a well-known woman. But, despite all that, every night, my mother told me how much she loved me and that I was her biggest treasure.

From the opened door, a tall, muscular man and a petite woman dressed in black and capes walked in.

"Where is she?" the man asked. He removed his hood and revealed long silver hair in a low ponytail. He scanned the room with his scary red eyes. "Tell me, woman! Where is she?"

He took a dagger from his belt, but the woman put a hand on his chest to stop him from doing anything he might do.

"Not so quick, babe. Let me first find the girl, and then we'll call Eris." Her voice was snaky and sour.

The woman had short silver hair and, just like her - husband? - scary red eyes.

"I'll go check the upstairs to see if the girl is there. You'll stay here; if she tries anything, kill her."

I swallowed hard. I walked backwards on my knees, under the table.

When the man wasn't paying attention, I saw my mother look in my direction. She smiled weakly and mimed with her lips I love you.

My heart started racing.

She put her hands behind and started a spell. In between her hands started forming a blue wave of magic. As she moved her fingers more, the wave became bigger and stronger. Even from how far I was, I could feel its power.

The man probably felt the power, too, because he turned my mother around and squeezed her hand until she fell on the floor in pain.

I tried not to scream and ran to her side. I knew it would've caused her even more pain if I did.

"SABEL!" he screamed at the woman upstairs.

I heard the woman's footsteps coming closer and closer. When she started going down the stairs, the man raised his dagger. He raised it above his head and, just like thunder striking, stabbed my mother right in the middle of the chest with it.

I screamed.

Both the man and the woman (Sabel) looked in my direction. I ran from under the table, took my satchel from the hanger, and ran through the back door with the man and woman behind me.

I woke up in my bed screaming.

My breath was still heavy from the nightmare.

The nightmare brought back all the feelings and pain I had. I didn't remember the things the man and woman said, I didn't remember the name of the woman either. I wanted to believe that the being that made me forget what they said made me forget it and remember it in this dream for a reason.

Nyx jumped on my lap and started purring.

"Good morning, kitty!"

I stayed in my bed with Nyx on my chest, looking at the ceiling. Then, judging by the sun's position, I made up that it was about ten in the morning, meaning I slept longer than usual.

As I stared at the ceiling more, I realized how blank it was. I looked at it for so much time since I found the meadow. I stared at it, thinking about how to spice it up.

Nyx moved and sat on my head, his tail on my face.

I stared at the ceiling and remembered the dream. I started thinking about Mom. She was the most powerful witch in the world. Everywhere she went, all the witches around looked at her with admiration, but that wasn't enough for my grandma. She wanted her to be the best at everything. Everything she made and did had to be perfect. She wanted my mother to marry a high rang man. That's why she went crazy when she learned that my mother was in love with a demon.

I remembered from what mom used to tell me that she was fourteen when she met my dad. He wasn't always a demon. At first, he was an ordinary boy with everyday life, but he got sick. The doctors said he didn't have more than a few weeks to live, but my dad made a pact with a demon to make him one as well and make his family and everyone who knew him forget him, so that they won't suffer. He lived as a demon for years until, one day, he met my mother. They met one night when my mother returned from the field where her family grew crops. He approached her in his demon form. My mother didn't run. She looked at him and saw all the pain and suffering he had gone through.

After that, they started seeing each other almost daily and never got sick of each other.

After two years of dating, she got pregnant - don't ask me how that was possible, as demons can't have biological children; my mother never told me. When my grandma found out, she was furious. She believed that witches and demons should be mortal enemies. Every day, she gave my aunt my mother as an example of what not to do. But she still didn't kick my mother out of the house.

I remember that my dad was around until I turned six; after that, I had never seen him again. Mom didn't know where he went. At the time, she was working multiple jobs a day, and I used to see her very little.

Suddenly, the idea of what to do with the ceiling came to me. The only problem was that I didn't have any paint.

I got out of bed and sat at the desk. I took a piece of paper from the drawer and started writing on it.

Dear Will,

Can you come and bring some of your paint and brushes with you? I have a really fun thing I want to do, and I would like to know if you will help me.

You don't have to send back a letter, Nyx will bring you the letter, and you can go with him; if not, you can give Nyx

I folded the paper and gave it to Nyx. "Get this to Will."

He jumped out of bed and went out the open window. I looked at him, circling the house and going out the meadow. When he was out of sight, I went to the counter and took a bowl out of it.

I put some yogurt I bought yesterday and some of the berries I had in a jar. Then, I sat at the table and started eating.

When I heard a knock at the door, I was reading one of the books I had read a hundred times on the couch.

I jumped from the couch and went to open the door.

Nyx started scratching my feet, telling me to pick him up.

"Hello!" said Will.

He was dressed in a beige-blue shirt and some brown pants. In his right hand, he was holding a wooden toolbox.

"I brought the paint and also some cookies," he added.

"Thanks." I stayed in the door awkwardly. Finally, I moved out of the door and let Will enter.

He placed the things he brought me on the kitchen table. His left palm and wrist were bandaged. When his left hand touched the table, he quickly took his hands off it, for the pain shook him hard.

"What happened to your hand?" I asked him.

"Nothing important."

There was no doubt in my mind that he was lying. He didn't even look me in the eye when he answered my question. He even had a different body language than usual, which seemed more mature. Despite only seeing each other a week ago (we sent letters to each other with the aid of some of my furry and winged friends), he already looked more mature than when we first met.

"What did you need the paint for?" he asked.

"I came up with this idea this morning," I said, taking my mind off that thought. "I want to paint the ceiling above my bed."

"Any ideas?"

"Yes, I actually have one."

I went to the couch and took a small drawing I'd been using as a bookmark out of the book. Then, instead of it, I put a piece of paper so I wouldn't lose the page I was on.

"I made this drawing with my mom when I was eight," I said, putting it on the table so that Will could see it too. "We were sitting one night on the roof of our house watching the stars. So when we came down, I drew what I saw in the stars."

Will took a notebook and some pencils out of the toolbox and started sketching something.

The picture was a constellation I had imagined. If the stars were traced together, you could see a young woman with a flower in her hands. Every night I look at the sky, I see my so-called constellation. It reminds me of my mother, which is why I want to paint it on the ceiling. So every night and morning, I could remember her.

I looked at the sketch Will was making. He moved his pencil like a simple dance he'd danced a thousand times, pressing the paper softly on some spots and harder on others.

He was drawing with the hand that was bandaged. On the palm, the bandage had a slight tint of maroon.

Nyx walked at my legs, making me lose my balance. I put a hand on Will's shoulder to keep my balance.

I teleported into a different location as soon as I touched his shoulder. The palace's training grounds were in front of me. Several boys and girls stood in front of me, Will among them. They were grouped into two-person teams.

The two girls were each with a boy, and Will was with Sebastian. The guards in training were on their own since there were no "teachers" on the grounds.

One of the boys that were grouped with a girl started arguing with Will, something I was too far away to hear. The boy had buzz-cut blond hair and fierce eyes. He pushed Will, making him back out.

The boy took his sword and started attacking Will. He hit Will, aiming for his legs first and then for his chest. Sapphires managed to block all his attacks, but when the boy aimed for his head - the sword horizontally placed - he leaned back, allowing his opponent to take Will's sword out of his hands. The opponent yanked the sword out of Will's hands, touching his hand with the blade, leaving a cut on his hand.

Sebastian (and the girl the boy was training with) tried stopping them, but the boy didn't stop. So instead, he attacked Will until he was on the ground with multiple cuts on his body.

Sebastian managed to stop the boy.

A "teacher" appeared on the field and saw what had happened. He sent Will and Sebastian somewhere inside the castle.

The image started fading, and I found myself back in my cabin.

"Lili, are you ok?" Will looked at me, worrying.

I snapped out of my trans. "Yeah... I-I'll be back in a sec."

I walked to the bathroom and shut the door. I washed my face and looked at myself in the mirror.

"How the heck did I do that?" I told myself silently. I didn't even want to activate that spell. Maybe because I was curious about what happened? That might be it... but still...

Let's talk about it, said a voice in my head that I recognized immediately.

I pinched the temple of my nose. "Hecate, not now, please."

She started appearing in the mirror like she was a reflection. She wore her usual silver moon diadem. This time she wore a long black dress with a low (very low) neckline and cut sleeves. The dress had some silver moons and stars drawn on the skirt of it.

"Now," she said. "We don't have much time, so let's talk."

"About what?"

"About what happened. You know that's not normal. That would keep happening as long as you keep all your magic in and channel it through the wand; it would happen more and more."

"So, what do you suggest? That I stop using my wand? You know that I can't cast spells without it."

"Of course, you can. You just don't want to," she said, her voice getting more firm.

"You know very well what happened last time!" I raised my voice without wanting to.

I turned my head at the big, wooden door. Will knocked on it and asked if I was all right.

"I'm fine," I told him in response.

When I turned my head back at the mirror, Hecate was gone.

After moving the bed to the side so we wouldn't stain it with the paint, we started sketching with pencils on the ceiling. We decided that we would paint only an area, like an opening to the night sky.

While I finished drawing small falling stars, Will mixed some paint and made a dark blue-purple color. He gave me a giant paintbrush and put the paint on a chair near us. Then, he got up on his chair and started painting the ceiling. He was more quiet than usual. Again, I was tempted to read his mind, this time intentionally.

"What's on your mind?" I asked him.

"Nothing," he responded weakly.

"Don't lie, Will!"

"Lili, there's nothing, trust me." Just like before, he didn't look at me when he told me that.

"Will!" I turned to him. "I can tell you're lying to me!"

There was yet to be a response from him.

As I painted the ceiling, I dipped my paintbrush into the night sky paint. I tried not to paint over the place where the stars were supposed to go. Instead, I changed the color to a lighter purple and painted the side of the "window" to look more three-dimensional.

The sun was still shining brightly on the sky, lighting up the entire cabin.

As time passed, I finished with the purple; I washed the paintbrush and took the white paint. I grabbed a cookie from the table and stuffed it in my mouth. I placed the paint on the chair and sat a little beside it.

As I was eating my cookie - which was very tasty, by the way - I looked at Will. His hair was full of blue paint. (I probably had paint in my hair too.)

"You want to know what is wrong?" he asked, getting off the chair.

I didn't say anything. I didn't even look at him.

"Five years ago today, my mom died. So that's what's happening, Flower."

He looked at me for a reaction. I did not know what to say.

"You don't need to say anything; your eyes say it for you," he looked at me.

"How did it happen? I mean, how did she die?" I said, pulling my chair closer to him.

"I don't know much about it. Dad never told me the details. Even the guards refused to tell me. I just know that she died in battle with the captain of an enemy troop. She separated from her troop and went to the enemy camp. The enemies caught her and killed her. Mom's troops found her body and took her to the castle. When Dad found out, he was destroyed. He told me about her death only a week later."

"Did they find the killer?" I looked up at his big sapphire eyes.

"Not to this day." He looked out the window in pain. "She taught me everything I know. She taught me how to paint and fight. Sometimes, I wouldn't see her for weeks. I used to look out my bedroom window and wait for her to return on her horse, Midnight."

He turned his head, facing me. "Dad made things even worse. After Mom's death, he started being distant and leaving for work trips for sometimes even months. I was lucky that Aunt Roseberry came by our house daily. Then, after a while, Dad started sending me to the castle to train so often - especially when he was away - that I couldn't even call my home "*home*". I have to pack my stuff and go to the castle for another month because Dad's on one of his trips."

"Then why are you here?" I asked him. "If you had to do something more important than help me paint the ceiling, you could've told me."

"I would've come anyway. You're my friend, Lili," he said, hugging me from the side.

I hugged him back. I put my head on his shoulder and looked at the pine trees outside the window.

"And you're mine, Will."

"What about we finish painting the ceiling?" he asked, getting up.

I nodded.

After we finished the painting, we moved the bed back and looked at the ceiling to see if we missed any spots.

"I think it looks great," I said.

Will was sitting on a chair at the table, eating some cookies. Nyx was probably somewhere outside - like he always is.

"Yeah," he said with his mouth full of cookies. "It looks really great."

I stared at the ceiling, looking at the painted stars, when Will said out of nowhere:

"You know? It's odd, the things you can remember when you find out that someone died."

I thought for a second. "It's even odder when you see them die in front of you."

"All the happy moments flash before your eyes; then, your life crushes before you."

"And then you realize you're on your own," I turned my head to the side, biting my lip.

Silence filled the room, but it wasn't the awkward type; it was more of a comfortable one.

I took a hair tie from the desk next to my bed and started playing with it. Being a witch, I always have to do something with my hands. It helps me concentrate. A lot of times, I play with my fingers or parts of my clothes. When my hair is longer, I play with it a lot.

I wrapped the hair tie in my fingers and unwrapped it. I rolled it on and out of my hand.

I could imagine almost perfectly a little Will looking out the window, waiting on the couch of his bedroom for his mom to arrive, only for her to never return.

Sometimes, I wonder why things like this happen to people who don't deserve it. This isn't about me. The things that happen to me happen for a reason, but people like Will don't deserve those kinds of things. His world probably felt like it was collapsing at the point he found out.

"But we don't have to be on our own anymore," I said, leaning on my elbows and looking at him. "We have each other now."

He smiled.

Chapter 14

I woke up to the smell of berries.

My eyes felt like heavy curtains. I didn't want to get out of bed, but I had to. Today was a big day.

I pushed the blanket to the side and got out of bed. On the table, I saw a light purple cake. I laughed softly.

As I got closer to the table, I saw some paper cards. I took one in my hand and read:

Happy fifteen, kid!

-Hades

I smiled. Hades and I go way back. He was the first god that I ever talked to. He helped me get out of many situations and get over even more things.

I took a look at the cake. The frosting had a light lilac color. It was nicely decorated and it made "waves" on the side and top. Small purple butterflies were scattered all over the cake.

Out of nowhere, the butterflies started flapping their wings and flinging off the cake. They flew around me, some remaining on my braided hair, some returning on the cake.

"Thank you," I said softly, knowing the gods would hear me.

I took my clothes and went to the bathroom.

Nyx was sleeping at the end of my bed, not moving a muscle. He would probably be somewhere with his animal friends in about an hour.

I started to unbraid my hair. French braids were one of my favorite ways to make my hair after washing it. When I unbraid them, my hair is left with beautiful waves.

I put on a puffy sleeve white shirt and a long dark green checkered dress. The material was thin enough so I won't sweat. Even though summer started two weeks ago, it was already hot outside.

I took some yogurt and berries from the kitchen cupboards - I eat this almost every morning - and put them in a bowl. I sprinkled some oatmeal over them and sat at the table. I told myself that I would eat the cake when I returned from the castle, mainly because I didn't want to eat cake as breakfast and because I was born just before midnight.

When the clock showed twelve o'clock, I took my satchel

and put on my brown high boots.

"I'll be back later," I told the cat as I left the cabin. I left the door intentionally open so that Nyx could go out.

The path I took was the one I usually walked on to get out of the woods. This road takes me to Will's village.

Just as always (in the day), the woods were gorgeous and quiet.

When I got to the village, Aunt Roseberry was gathering some flowers from the side of the road.

"Good day, Miss Roseberry!" I told her.

"Good day to you too, Lili!" she said, turning to me. "How are you doing, sweetie?"

"I'm great. I'm headed for the festival. What about you?"

"You know, just the usual things. I'll go later to the festival, too."

She came closer to me and gave me a bouquet of white, pink, and purple anemones. "Happy birthday, sweetie!"

And she started walking towards the village.

"But... how did you... how did you..." but she was too far away to hear me.

I smelled the flowers. The sweet smell of the flowers went straight through my nostrils and filled my lungs.

When I got to the city, the sound of joy was unavoidable. As I walked the street, the music got louder and louder. Most people gathered around the fountain and along the road to the castle entrance.

The castle gates were fully opened, letting all the town people walk inside the castle area. So if I wanted to meet Elizabeth, that's the way I had to go.

I put some flowers in my hair and ran my hand over the rest of them, making them disappear. Later, when I return to the meadow, I'll find them on the table, next to the cake, just as fresh as when Aunt Roseberry gave them to me.

"Lili," said the voice of Elizabeth from next to me. She wore her flowery cape with her hood on, not letting people see who she was. "In three hours, the 'royal' party guests will enter the castle."

"Won't they notice I'm not royal?" I whispered.

She looked around. "Can you use the invisibility spell on yourself?"

"Yeah, of course."

"You'll walk past the guards inside the castle," she gave me a piece of paper and unfolded it, revealing the floor plans of the castle.

"My room is here," she showed me a big room on the castle's third floor. "I'll leave the door open for you to enter. If I'm not there, don't panic, I'll come. Understand?"

I nodded.

"Ok then, I will see you later."

Before she could get away, I told her, "Happy birthday!"

"Thanks," she smiled.

I turned and saw her getting lost between the people on the street.

My eyes changed direction and saw Will and Sebastian looking at me. I cursed silently.

They started walking toward me. I told myself repeatedly that they didn't see me talking to Elizabeth, but unfortunately, that wasn't the case.

"Was that Elizabeth?" asked Sebastian.

"Elizabeth? Do you mean the princess? No! No, of course not. That wasn't her." I said nervously.

"You sure? I gave her that cape last year for her birthday."

Will stayed silent, listening to Sebastian ask questions. He glared at me, his sapphire eyes telling me he knew I was lying.

"I'm telling you, that wasn't the princess. Maybe there is someone else that has the same cape."

"It can't be. That cape was custom-made for her," he looked at me skeptically.

162

"You know?" said Will. "Just leave it. It really doesn't matter. What about we go and get something from Patty's?"

"Yeah, sure. Let's go get something to eat," said Sebastian, walking in front of us.

I moved to Will's side when Sebastian was a few meters away.

"Thank you so much!" I told him.

"Any time. Will you tell later what that was about?"

"Later," I said to him as we walked behind Sebastian. At the moment, I didn't intend to tell Will about what I was doing.

When we went out of Patty's, I heard music playing. I looked at where the music was playing and saw a young girl playing the guitar and some girls dancing.

I ate the rest of the croissant I got before dragging Will over to where the music was coming from. The girl playing the guitar was non-other than my coworker Ivy.

A girl around the same age as the one who played the guitar started pulling a few people to dance. Soon, she saw me and took hold of my hand. She pulled me in and danced with me for a little bit. Then, we all switched partners, and I could see Will still outside the circle, staring at me with a bright smile.

"Come on, Sapphs!" I called him from the dancing circle.

He shook his head; no, but someone had other plans. Ivy was accompanied by a boy who also played the guitar, allowing her to take a small break and pull some people into the circle to dance. After she pulled Will in, she started playing the guitar again.

I laughed and watched him get taken away by someone. Now I was dancing with Sebastian. He spun me a couple of times before he got pulled by someone else.

I saw the little red-headed girl on the side of the dancing circle. She sat close by Miss Miliani. I walked to her and asked the girl if she would dance with me. She nodded delicately, taking my hands. I spun her around, making her giggle. She wore a simple cream dress that made her fire-red hair pop.

I made a flower appear in my hand, just like the ones Aunt Roseberry gave to me, and put it in her hair.

"How did you...?" she said with a sweet soft voice.

"I'll tell you soon," I said before giving her back to where she first sat.

After I danced with a few other people, I ended up with Will. The person I last danced with pushed me into his chest (probably smashing one of his ribs). I could feel my cheeks heat up and probably turn dark red.

"I swear, if you used magic to get me in here, I'd never forgive you," he said, but I could tell he was joking just by his tone.

"Trust me, if I had used magic, you would've known," I smirked up at him. He was way taller than me. I turned my head to the side but saw from the corner of my eye that he was smiling.

After we danced a little longer, Will pulled me out of the circle and dragged me onto a side street.

"Where are we going?" I asked him.

"You'll like it."

I was getting the déjà vu feeling. Once again, he dragged me through the entire city to a place I did not know.

We walked the empty streets, the music starting to fade.

Will took me to a hill that was just ten minutes away from the city.

Somewhere along the hill, I took off my boots and walked without them on the soft grass.

"Next time you want to take me up a hill," I told him, a little out of breath. "Please send me a letter not to put on boots. My muscles will hurt like crazy by the time I get back to the meadow."

He turned around and looked at me. "I didn't even know you were coming."

"It's not like I had a choice," I said more for myself, but Will heard and looked at me like I would look at a geometry problem.

(I do learn things like geometry, algebra, and all those things. Hades insisted that I had to.)

Will stopped a few meters away from me. The view from up here was breathtaking. I could see every street and every garden. I could see the fountain and the crowd that danced and crowded to see the court and all the royalties to come.

"It's beautiful!"

"I told you you'll like it."

I looked once more at the view and put my boots on the ground.

"We didn't finish dancing," I told Will.

"We didn't?" he asked with a smirk.

"We didn't."

He got closer, and I felt a hand on my waist and another holding my hand. I looked up at his blue eyes. He spun me around and pulled me back upon his chest. I almost tripped over my boots, but Will caught me. We both giggled and continued dancing.

He spun me a few more times, and when he wasn't paying attention, I spun him, too, making him smile.

I could only stare into his sapphire eyes and smile up at him. He, too, smiled down at me, his cute dimples showing.

He picked me up by my waist with one arm and turned us around. I couldn't control my laughter, and neither could he. He placed me back on the ground, and we continued dancing, large smiles on our faces.

Will twirled me out, facing the city, and then I twirled back into him. I ended up right against his chest. We both stayed there for a moment before Will pulled away.

He looked to the side of the castle, not meeting my eyes. We both had blushes on our cheeks and noses.

The silence between us was unbearable, suffocating.

I looked at the city. I saw the carriages arrive.

Shit.

I hurried and put my boots on.

"See you at the meadow later?"

He didn't answer.

"Yes? That's great! See you!"

I started running down the hill, with Will in the back, asking where I was in such a hurry. I left him standing there, hoping to see him later in the meadow.

I ran like my life depended on it.

The streets were still as empty as people saying that children go to school for pleasure.

When I got into the main area, where the dancing circle played earlier, the people were crowded like ants on a piece of apple. I could barely get through them.

"Sorry," I said to a short man who carried bags. "Sorry!"

The people were so crowded that they made a human dam for other humans. There was no other way to cross the streets, so I got on my hands and knees and crawled under them.

Then the people started pushing each other; I made myself invisible and ran straight through them. Smart move? Of course not.

When I got to the castle entrance, I sat with my back on a carriage, catching my breath. I looked to the side, seeing the castle doors. The doorkeeper started closing the doors.

I ran in front of the horses and sprinted between the doors, sliding on the side.

I was in.

Chapter 15

I took out the map that the princess gave me.

I was at the main entrance. With my finger, I found the closest stairs leading me to the third floor. The only problem is that it was the way all the people that entered the castle were walking on.

I walked on the side of the blue rug next to the wall.

The last time I'd been inside the castle, I walked straight ahead of the entrance and went up a different set of stairs. This time, at the door, I turned right.

In the hallway, from twenty to twenty meters, there were round glass tables with silver edges, each with a vase full of colorful flowers.

I stopped in front of a big open door. The room was full of people dressed in elegant clothes. On a stage, in the back of the room, I saw the King, Queen, and Elizabeth. The silence overfilled the room. The king spoke.

"I thank you all for coming to the celebration of my daughter's sixteen birthday," and he continued, but I was already at the stairs, losing the sound of his voice.

The upstairs was almost empty. The only people there were a few guards, and all were heading my way.

They passed right by me.

As I walked, I looked around for any more guards. They all went down. I don't understand what kind of guarding system this is. Leaving an entire floor free of guards? They might not have that many thieves around Lovskaria.

The doors of Elizabeth's bedroom were huge. They were white, with baby blue details. I looked again in the hallway, opened the doors, and entered the room.

My eyes had to adjust to the powerful light that filled the room. The windows were the size of a decent size living room. They had curtains the color of the ice over a clean blue river.

The floor was made out of a light-colored wood - maybe maple wood - most of it covered by carpet that matched the color of the curtains. The only place you could see the wooden floor was the small platform on which a desk, an easel, and a bookshelf sat.

Next to the platform were a few guitars and violins.

And next to the instruments, a big archway led into a dressing room with walls full of clothes. In the middle of it was put a long tabouret.

The bed was placed on the wall opposite the archway to

the dressing room.

The bed was bigger than a king-size one. It was a canopy bed with elegant drapes. The bed sheets were light pink. The pillows filled the bed. They were all different colors that shouldn't go with the room, but somehow, the colors were perfect.

On the wall that the bed sat against, splashes of paint filled the wall. It looked unintentional, but at the same time, it looked like a piece of art the most famous artist would do.

I took a look through the windows. My feet walked to the balcony, and my hands opened the door. The summer breeze made my hair dance and my lips smile.

A couple of birds sang on the railing, filling the place with their mesmerizing song.

I walked to the edge and looked down. The view wasn't as beautiful as it was from the hill, but it was still lovely. For sure a royal view.

My eyes flew over Will. He was heading for the training grounds. Or at least it seemed like he was.

Why am I disappointed he didn't... he didn't kiss me?

My eyes moved to the horizon, losing my gaze on him.

My heart was in different places at once. *Maybe I should forget that ever happened.*

I went back inside and made myself visible again.

For a second, I thought about getting back into the castle and finding what I needed. I didn't know what I would need from the castle, I just had the feeling that I needed the map, but I was sure that Elizabeth would take it back.

I took some papers from the princess's desk and put them over the maps she gave me. Then, I started tracing the walls and doors. When I finished a room, I wrote down which one it was. It took a while to finish drawing them. Every time I heard a sound, I panicked and gathered the papers.

When I got to write the name of a room in the basement, I stopped. The name of it played in my mind. *The Room of Magic*. And it played and played.

"The Room of Magic," I whispered to myself. I like the name of it. Mysterious.

When I finished drawing, I put the papers in my satchel and looked again at the original floor plan. When I drew Elizabeth's room, I saw a door I couldn't find in the actual room.

I looked around. The door in the floor plan wasn't the one that led into the room, nor the one to the bathroom. It wasn't the archway either.

The mysterious door was marked right where the wall had paint splashes. I got closer and moved my hand above it. I felt magic.

The Room of Magic.

"Who are you?" asked a voice.

I turned and saw a girl. She looked a few years older. Her hair was cut to her shoulders, and half was pinned. It had the color of rich soil. Her brown locks were shining in the light. The underlayer of her hair had the color of sand. She was dressed in a light green dress with golden details. If anything, she didn't look like she was part of the royal family. They all wore blue and gold.

"Lili," said Elizabeth coming into the room, her voice tight. "And, Aideen... What are you doing here, Aideen?"

"I was looking for you. You disappeared from your own party," Aideen said with her voice clear, not moving her eyes off me. "Now, who is she?"

"She's Lili. Lili, this is Aideen, my best friend."

"And what's she doing here?" asked the girl.

Elizabeth hesitated. "You know the nightmares I told you about? The ones that keep repeating? The ones with that woman? Lili might be able to help me with them."

"How can she help you?" she said, her voice getting convened.

Elizabeth turned to me. Her eyes told me to trust Aideen, but my gut told me not to. I had to help the princess, so I had to trust Aideen.

"I'm a witch. I know about dreams. And I know a thing or two about Eris," I said, approaching the two.

"You're a witch? An actual witch?"

I nodded.

"But you don't look like one?" Aideen said.

"Witches aren't as ugly as people think," I said with a dead tone in my voice. I am tired of people thinking that all witches have to be ugly.

"How are you going to help Liz?"

"Did you have any more dreams?"

"Last night. That," she pointed to the wall with splashed paint, "is the result of last night's nightmare. But, unfortunately, ever since I last saw you, the nightmare's been getting worse and more frequent."

"I already looked at the wall. Nothing special," I lied. "Anything else?"

She walked to the desk and, from the bookcase next to it, she took a book.

I went next to her.

"I've been writing the nightmares from the past year here. Every detail. You can read from it," said the princess, giving me the book.

I took it and opened it to the first page.

May 16

It happened again. She was sitting on the edge of the bed. I screamed, but not a word came out of my mouth. She rose and walked to my side.

I tried moving, but I was glued to my bed; hands, legs, everything.

She put her hand on my mouth. I tried biting her.

"Now, now. Don't do that. No, no. You'll do what I want you to, and you'll be a good girl. And don't say any of this to the witch."

And I woke up.

Aideen was telling Elizabeth something that she had to do later. Something about Aideen made me think she was not to trust, but if the princess said she was her best friend, she couldn't have been that bad. After all, my gut feeling might have been wrong, wouldn't be a first.

As the girls talked, I read some of the passages. Most of them were of Eris telling Elizabeth to listen to her and do what she wants. But, in all of them, she told her not to trust me. None of them were Eris telling her what she wanted Elizabeth to do. And in many of them, Eris said things that didn't make sense. Things that didn't work together.

June 13

I got out of bed and went to the desk. Just like most of the nights, I couldn't sleep. So I took a brush and started painting on my easel. I dipped the brush in green paint.

When I wanted to change the color, I saw that the can of blue paint was empty.

I went to the cart in which I had my paints and looked for the blue I wanted.

From behind my back, I heard a sound. I turned to see what it was. My eyes flew over nothing, but I saw her when I turned my head.

Her appearance made me fall over the cart of paint. The paint splashed all over the wall and floor.

The woman floated closer to me. She followed me all around the room, always appearing in front of me.

I made a wrong move. I ran into the corner, and she blocked me.

"I leave signs, my dear. Be careful."

She came closer and crouched. Her milky white eyes stare into my soul. When she reached her hand to touch me, I woke up in my bed on the morning of my birthday.

I glanced at the wall. Its only colors were purple, green, blue, and yellow.

From my satchel, I took a blank piece of paper.

"Is it ok if I take a pen to write something?" I asked the princess.

"Sure."

On the paper, I noted all the colors on the wall. I also noted the things Eris said, all the things she said from May sixteen to last night.

When I wrote the last thing she said, my pen stopped.

'I leave signs.'

Why do gods and demons have to speak like this? Never telling things straight.

"Did you figure out anything?" Elizabeth asked.

"Not yet, but I think Eris wants you to lose your strong will and fall for her lies. Don't. We're just pawns in Eris's game. Suppose the dreams start including anyone else, Sebastian, Aideen - anyone. Come to me," I took a small pause. "I'll give you some charms and things that might protect you from Eris. For now, I can give you an amethyst neckless."

I took from my satchel the "backup" neckless. "Take it as a birthday present. If I figure anything out, I'll send a letter to Will to give to you."

"Will?" Aideen turned to face me. "How do you know Will?"

"Long story."

I walked to the desk and took the paper. I touched the notebook and made a short spell.

"If you want to come and spend some time here, you are allowed here. You're my friend, Lili; you don't need the invitation to come."

"Thank you," I said softly.

As I put the paper in my satchel, I saw Aideen look at me, frozen.

"You are the girl Will's talking about," said Aideen.

My legs froze on my way to the door. I ignored what she said.

"Happy birthday, Elizabeth!" I told her as I was making myself invisible.

"How do you do that?" asked the girl.

"I was invisible too," said Elizabeth to her friend. They started talking, forgetting I was even there.

Chapter 16

I decided to walk back to my meadow. I could've just teleported myself inside of it, but I felt like I shouldn't.

The town was still busy. I walked slowly, taking my time.

The maze of people speeded on the streets. After a few minutes of walking, I was alone on the road. Only from a distance, I could hear voices. The sound was diffused, my mind taking over.

Eris doesn't play. Everything she says and does is part of some plan of hers. I need to figure out what she wants. I need to figure out why the princess is involved in her plan.

The colors have meaning. So when I get to the meadow, I'll look in one of the books to see what I can find about color.

All I knew was that this wouldn't end with Eris winning.

I left my satchel on the coat hanger.

My legs were hurting from all the walking. I knew that I was going to walk a lot today. Unfortunately, I made a bad decision again.

I collapsed on the table chair. The cake looked the same as I left it. Next to it, the flowers were put in a vase.

I didn't know I could do this with my magic.

When I first came to the meadow, in the same vase, I found flowers. Even though the furniture inside the cabin had at least a centimeter of dust on it, the flowers were still fresh.

That was one of the many mysteries of the meadow.

I took the birthday card from the table and looked at it once again. Even though Hecate was my guide, Hades was the one who set up the cake and the card. He was the one who cared about my life outside of the "magic" world. Hecate only cared about making my magic and me more powerful. To me, it didn't seem that Hecate actually cared about me.

A little tear fell out of my eye. And that tear was followed by another one. I wiped them with my fingers. I wasn't going to cry on my birthday.

"When were you going to tell me it is your birthday?"

"Will?" I said, wiping my eyes.

I saw him standing on the edge of my bed, playing with Nyx. I don't understand how I didn't see him or how I didn't feel that he was in the room.

"How long have you been here?" I asked him.

"Long enough for a book to fall on my head from the ceiling," he joked.

I smiled. "So, for about an hour and a half."

"Back to my question?" he got up and came to the table, leaving Nyx to play with a ball of thread.

"I didn't think you'd care."

"Of course I care, Flower! Why would you think I don't care?"

"I learned that the people I care about don't care about me; my grandma, my guide..."

"I thought you didn't have any family left."

"I have a grandmother, an aunt, and a cousin, but I haven't seen them in years. A year before Mom's death, she argued with my grandma. She said some horrible things about my father and me. Finally, my mother couldn't take it anymore. She loved her sister, but we no longer went to their house. We already lived in different villages. I miss hanging out with my cousin."

This was a part of the story I wanted to forget. It hurt telling it, but at the same time, I felt like it was helping.

"I thought my grandparents said some bad things," he said.

"Your grandparents don't see the whole story. But, once they get the whole picture, I'm sure they'll understand."

My grandma knew the entire story but still didn't stop saying bad things. She used to tell me things like I wasn't worth it, I ruined my mother's life, I didn't deserve to be here, that I was a disappointment just as big as my mother, and that if it wasn't for me, my mother would've been a famous witch. She said things that, for a child, hurt worse than any other thing she could've ever done.

"Why are you crying?" Will asked with concern in his voice.

I didn't even realize I was crying. It was a silent, painful cry.

"That's a part of my life I want to forget."

"I'm sorry I've asked."

"It's all right. I'm better now," I said, brushing away a tear. "What do you say about eating some cake? I'll go take the plates."

On the table, next to the cake, were some candles. Will took them and put them on the cake. Then, he started singing *Happy Birthday* to me.

For the first time in a long time, I was truly happy. The smile on my face was big and real. The laughs were full.

Will took Nyx and moved his paws, making it seem

like Nyx was singing. This made me crack a few smiles. However, the cat's face told me he would pay for this.

I cut the cake and put it on the plates. It tasted like fresh strawberries, my favorites.

"I don't know how you made this cake, but it's delicious," said Will, stuffing his mouth with it.

"I didn't make it. Hades did. He's actually a really great cook," I told him.

"Of what knowledge I have of Greek mythology, isn't Hades the god of the underworld?"

Shit.

"Yeah, uh, I've been wanting to tell you this for a while," I tried to play it cool even if it wasn't. "You know about the Greek gods, but did you know that they are very much still alive?"

"No. I- I didn't know." He looked like everything he ever knew was turning up to be fake. "And they walk the earth?"

"Well, not anymore. At least not in the shape witches see them."

"So, witches can see gods?"

"Mostly, we can see them in dreams and visions. They sometimes appear in real life."

From the couch, I could see a pillow move. "And we can feel when they're in the same room. So you can come out, Hades."

On the couch, a dark-skinned man with cornrow braids looked at Will and me. He wore a black suit with a golden accent on the buttons.

Hades waved at us. I saw Will's face turn white. He blinked a couple of times and slid down the chair, falling to the ground.

I jumped off my chair and went to see if Will was fine.

"Nice! He fainted!"

I checked if he was breathing, which he was. Then, I loosened his collar and laid him on his back.

I sat next to his head.

Hades moved from the couch to the table. He looked down at Will.

"He's breathing, right?" asked the god.

"He is," I looked up at him.

"That's great. I didn't want Persephone to beat me up for scaring another person to death," he says, arranging his suit.

I looked at him with big eyes. "You scared people to death? You know what? I don't even want to know!"

"That's good. I didn't think you want to."

"What are you doing here?" I asked him, but I was staring at Will.

"I came to say Happy Birthday to my favorite mortal," he said, spreading his arms. "Happy birthday, kid!"

"Thanks," I said, smiling. "And thank you for the cake. You baked it, right?"

"Of course I did. And may I add that Persephone didn't help me this year."

"That's good to know."

I looked at Will. His hair was pushed back, not covering his forehead. Not going to lie; it was the first time I saw his forehead.

"How'd you meet him?"

"Like you don't know," I said, looking at the god. "You follow every step I make."

"I do follow everything you make and do, but I don't look at everything you make and do. So there's a difference."

I rolled my eyes.

Since I was very little, Hades followed every step I made. Literally, he was the first to see me take my first steps. Then, my mother came home and saw me walk around the living room while Hades sat on the couch looking after me.

So almost every time he appears, he somehow correlates to that memory.

"And I think you should tell him about what's happening with the princess and Eris."

I saw Will's eyes open.

"What... what..."

"It's all right," I told him softly. "Stay there. I'll check in a moment if you have any head injuries."

He looked dizzy and out of place. His eyes moved all over the room, stopping on Hades.

"You are..." he tried saying, but I stopped him before ending his sentence.

After he stopped feeling dizzy, I gave him a glass of water.

"Hades?" I looked at the god while checking if Will had any head injuries.

"I'm sorry for making you faint," said the god like a child.

"It's all right, man. God? It-it's all right."

"You can get up, Sapphires," I told him as I sat on the chair.

He put his glass on the table and got up. He moved his chair, so he was closer to me and sat further away from

Hades.

"I don't bite, kid. Ask Butterfly," he said, raising his arms like he offered peace.

"Butterfly?"

"I used to make myself butterfly wings out of paper," I said fast, cutting both of their words.

I heard a large sound coming from behind me. Nyx pushed a book off the bed. When I went to lift it up, I saw that it was the one I had copied from Elizabeth's room.

I threw the book on the table and told Will about Eris and Elizabeth.

I couldn't describe Will's face better than Hades did.

"You look like Lili's mother when she saw me sitting on her living room couch watching Lili walk for the first time."

I told you he could reference that memory in any discussion. So I am sure he somehow manages to reference it even when Hades talks to Zeus or any other god.

"I promised I'll tell you this, and I also promised to tell you what Eris wants from me, but I never told you. So I'll tell you now. It's actually quite simple. Eris wants my powers. She wants me to suffer."

"Why?" asked Will turning his head at me.

"Because she's the only one who can destroy Eris," said Hades becoming serious. "The butterfly we have here is special. She's the first witch born out of a witch and a demon. Her powers are bigger than the whole sky."

I could feel Will's eyes on me when Hades said the part about my dad. I didn't tell him about my father for a reason. I don't expect people to feel that good around me if I tell them my father is a demon.

"Anyway," I said, deviating from the subject. "The thing is that Eris wants me dead before I find a way to get her dead."

"That's why those demon shape-shifters tried killing us?"

"Yes."

"That feels like ages ago."

"Doesn't it?" I smiled.

"Not to ruin your moment, but I just remembered. Lili" said Hades with concern in his voice. "You should be careful. The Hunters are coming to Lovskaria."

"No! No! No, they... no!" I got up from my chair. "I-I'm going to go get some air."

I walked up the hill and sat on the blanket, holding my knees. When I closed my eyes, the flashback started. The same day that my mother died. The ones who killed her are after me, too, now. They might not be in this part of the kingdom, but that doesn't mean they don't know I'm here.

I'll have to watch every one of my steps. Trust people only if my gut tells me to. Be careful of my words and actions. Never telling anyone else what I am. I might even need to resign from working for Miss Miliani.

I looked up at the sky. Time passed fast enough for the sky to turn from sapphire to indigo.

"I know you're up there, Mom," I told the stars. "I know you're looking after me, but it's not the same as having you next to me."

"I thought I was the only one who talked to stars."

Next to me appeared Will. "Can I sit here?"

I nodded.

"What's the matter?"

"Nothing," I said. "It's nothing."

"Lili! Be honest."

"It's just a matter of time until they'll find me, Will. It's just a matter of time until I'll get killed and until Eris wins. I can't even make a stupid spell do what it's supposed to!" I said, throwing my wand into the river. "At this point, I'm thinking about letting Eris kill me. At least then, I'll be with my mother again."

"It can't be that bad."

"The Hunters are the ones who killed my mother, Will! When I thought I had found a place where I could feel safe and sound, The Hunters appeared out of nowhere! I only wanted to find a place to feel at home again. When I finally found one, I find out that even more people who want to kill me are in the kingdom. It's the best birthday gift I could ever wish for!"

"I won't let them kill you, Lili." He looked into my eyes. "I promise."

I knew no one could protect me from Eris. The only one who could be me. I started this journey on my own, and it will end on my own. I'm OK with it.

"Thanks," I said.

From the cabin, I saw Hades come out the door. He met my gaze and started walking up the hill.

He straightened his suit and looked down at me. "Before I go, I need to give you this."

He made the green things I gave Hecate a while back appear out of thin air. "The broken one had let out Eris' soul."

"What?" I shouted, getting up almost immediately.

"Whoever broke this one has Eris inside. If I were you, I would go..."

"Thanks for everything, Hades! Tell Persephone I say hi to her. I'll see you next time! Bye!"

I started running down the hill, but when I got to the woods, I realized it would take too long to reach where I needed to.

"I'll leave them on the table!" shouted Hades.

Will ran next to me. "Where are you going?"

"I need to get to the tree trunk. Who knows what could be in others if Eris was in one of the things!"

"I'll go with you."

"Ok." I took his hand and, for the first time without my wand, I made a spell.

It wasn't that different from using a wand. The spell worked the same. The only difference was the tingling I had in my hand.

As the fume started disappearing, I saw the tree trunk in front of me.

I ran and removed the wood from the tree trunk.

"No... no..." I cried.

The spheres were gone. All of them. Eris made a move, and it worked. She's one step closer to winning the game.

I sure am.

I could practically hear her smirking. She was once again

in my head.

'I swear that if you don't get out, I'm going to....'

You're going to what? Kill me? You're not prepared enough for that. All you can do is listen to me.

The venom in her words spread all inside me. I could feel her cold presence surround me, the same one I felt when I met her in the woods. She was ready to strike again.

"Lili... What is that?" asked Will with fear in his voice.

"Stay back," was the last thing I told him before all I could see was black.

Chapter 17

He took the witch into his arms. He didn't know what had happened, but he knew that he needed to get Lili somewhere safe.

He walked as fast as he could. He had two choices. To get the girl to his house or to get her to the castle. Things would've turned way different if he had gone for his house.

The only people that were up in the town gave Will weird looks. No one questioned what he was doing or where he was heading to.

The boy went for the entrance to the training grounds. The guard there recognized him, so he let him go.

He didn't stop for a second, even if his legs were about to fall off. He wouldn't have stopped even if all the guards had tried to stop him.

Will wandered the castle until he found someone. Walked the corridors until he found the ballroom. Someone had to be there.

Fortunately, in the room were the princess and Sebastian. When Will entered the room, they were sitting at a table, flirting with each other. When they heard the doors open, their heads turned. They jumped off their seats and rushed to Will.

"What happened?" asked Elizabeth.

"I need help," was all Will said.

Sebastian turned to his girlfriend. "I'll go get Phrona. You get Will to the closest room possible."

"Come after me," said the princess.

They walked the hallways, trying to find an empty room.

Will looked down at Lili. Fortunately, she was breathing, but she didn't seem fine at all. Her face was as white as snow, making her freckles pop. She looked almost dead.

"What happened?" asked Elizabeth.

"Eris."

The princess stopped midway down the hallway. She looked frozen in place.

"Lili told you about Eris?"

"She told me a while ago."

The princess didn't say anything else. Instead, she took a turn to the left and then stopped. She looked at the doors, then turned to face Will.

"In that room," she showed to a door that was opened on the right wall. "I will go get Sebastian and Phrona here."

Will walked to the room. He placed the witch on the bed under the window and looked at her. He wished out of his entire heart for her to be fine. He never had a friend like her. Will felt like Lili understood him on the next level more than anyone else. She wasn't like other girls. She was something else, something different. In a way, Lili reminded Will of his mother. From the first moment he saw her, he knew she would mean more to him than others.

"What happened?" asked the voice of an older woman.

Will knew he couldn't tell her the truth. "I didn't see. I was searching for something I dropped, and when I turned, I saw her drop to the ground."

"Move to the side," said the woman. "I'll have to check her."

The woman asked them to get out of the room.

"What did Eris do to her?" asked the princess after closing the door to the room. Her voice was low and quiet, and at the same time, she was shouting.

"Who is Eris?" asked Sebastian.

"I'll explain to you later, Seb. What did she do?"

"I don't know. Dark-colored fume started surrounding her, and the moment it was all gone, she fell to the ground. The only one who knows is Lili."

Silence filled the room. Elizabeth's eyes had a spark in them like an idea came to her mind.

"There might be someone else that knows. Seb, stay here with Will. I'll be back as soon as I can."

The princess gave Sebastian something, and he put it in his pants pocket. Then, he looked after the girl until she disappeared. She was still dressed in the blue dress she had worn for her birthday.

"Who is Eris?" asked Sebastian trying to get answers.

"I know only little about her, only what Lili told me. She knows best. Elizabeth might know something too, but I don't think she knows as well as her."

"I'm not getting answers until she wakes up?"

"I think so."

They both sat on the floor, staring at the ceiling.

Will was so tired he could fall asleep right there. He hasn't done so many things in a day since he was a child. His muscles were sore. He could feel a headache creeping into his head. He felt his eyes close several times but forced himself to stay awake.

He thought about whom the princess wanted to bring to keep his mind awake. A witch, maybe. That was the only reasonable answer. So, of course, Will only knows about Lili, but there were many more witches in the kingdom.

Thinking about that made Will wonder how many witches he might know. For all he knew, everyone he had ever met could be a witch.

That made his head hurt more.

"How did you meet Lili?" asked Sebastian.

"Not so different from this," responded Will. "I found her in the woods, passed out. She was full of wounds. I couldn't leave her in the forest to die."

"And you didn't vomit all over the place?"

"No," he took a break. "Maybe once."

A few minutes passed, and the woman came out of the room.

"She'll need a lot of rest," she said first. "And I'll need her name."

"Lili. Actually, Lilium," responded Will.

"A really nice name she has, but I'll also need her family name. And to know where her parents are."

"Grace. Her family name is Grace."

"And her parents?"

Before Will could come up with a lie, Sebastian saved him. "It's better to talk with the king about that."

"I can't disturb the king at this late hour," said the offended woman.

"Then you can talk to him tomorrow morning. Thanks for checking on our friend. Good night, ma'am!"

"How dare you!" said the woman to Sebastian as she walked down the hallway.

They decided not to talk about it. Instead, the boys walked inside the bedroom.

Lili was lying on her back on the bed. Her hair was arranged beautifully on the pillow, like rays of sunshine. Her face was still as white as snow, but her lips started regaining their color.

The woman probably took off her boots because now they were on the floor, by the bed.

Will couldn't believe it was still the same day it was this morning. Things started way better. He had an excellent breakfast and a lovely morning walk through the castle gardens. Then he went to the festival in the princesses' honor and met with Lili. They danced and had a blast. Then he went and celebrated her birthday and even ate cake. He hadn't had cake in years. He never thought this was how the day would end in a thousand years.

And yet, from the moment he met her, he knew he wouldn't see things in pastel hues.

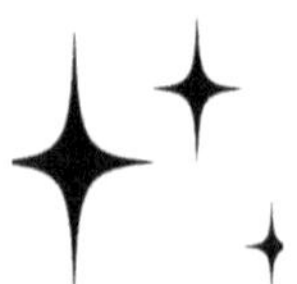

Will stayed with Lili for days, waiting for her to wake up. He only left for food and to bring Nyx to be near Lili.

The woman came and checked her every day. Finally, she said that Lili would be all right, that she needed rest, and that she could wake up any moment.

Even with all that, Will knew something was happening inside Lili's head. He knew she wouldn't wake up until Eris or whatever spell was put on her was broken.

One day Will remembered what the princess said when he brought Lili to the castle. So he walked all around the court, trying to find Elizabeth.

He didn't expect to find the princess training with Sebastian on the training grounds. It was a Sunday, so no one was supposed to be training.

"I don't want to ruin your training, Elizabeth, but I remember you saying that you know someone who might know what happened to Lili," said Will.

Elizabeth turned to him. "The guards didn't find her at her house. Most of the time, she's out in town."

"Could you please send them again? Please, Elizabeth!" pleaded Will.

"Only if you're going to plead on your knees," smirked the girl.

Will looked at her with a death stare, but he was ready to

get on his knees.

"I'm just kidding! I already sent some guards this morning."

When Will saw who came into the room, he dropped everything he had in his hands. His food, his book. All were on the floor.

The guards brought a short woman with dark skin and silver hair.

"Will," she said. "It's nice to see you."

"Aunt Roseberry," said Will losing his words. "What are you doing here?"

"Those lovely guards came to my house and told me the princess wanted me here. I couldn't say no to the princess."

"So you are..."

"I thought you'd figure this out faster. Especially after you met Lili," she said, sitting on the armchair. "So, what happened to her?"

For Will, it was a little too much to take in. His mind couldn't believe that the woman who used to stay with him every time his parents were away was a witch.

Now that he knew, he understood some of the weird things that happened around her and the things she did.

It was all clear. He didn't understand how he didn't figure this out before.

"Eris," when Will said the name of the demon Rosemary's face turned sour. "She somehow attacked Lili using some black fume. She hasn't woken up in days, and I don't think it's because she needs rest."

"Don't worry. I can get whatever is inside of her head out. It's not that complicated of a spell."

She got up from the armchair and went to the young witch. She placed her hands above her head and stayed like that. Her eyes turned white. She didn't say a word, but her lips were moving.

She finished and walked to the door. "She should wake up in less than two days. When she awakes, send the lovely guards to me; we'll talk more then."

Two days later, Lili awoke.

Thank you!

I want to thank many people for helping me with this book. Most of them don't even know how they helped me. Most of them had no idea that I was writing this story.

The only people who knew I was writing this book were my mother, father, and brother, and I want to thank them with my whole heart. They've been with me through the entire process of this book and every other project of mine. They helped me with more than they could imagine.

I want to thank my *English tutor, Ivona,* for helping me learn English. Without her, I wouldn't have written this book in English.

I also want to thank my primary school teacher for giving me the opportunity of writing a 'book' as a school project. (I took that project very seriously and created my first cooking book.) Without her, I wouldn't have discovered what I wanted to be.

I want to thank all my true and long-known friends for teaching me what a true friend is and inspiring many characters and situations in my stories.

And I also want to thank all the excellent writers whose books I've read and who made me want to make others happy with my books.

Constantin Chiriţa is a Romanian writer who wrote my all-time favorite book series: Cireşarii. But he isn't the one I want to thank. The person I want to thank is my father, who gave me this book series and allowed me to realize how happy and good books can make people feel.

Basically, I want to thank everyone I know, even if I like them or not, even if you're my friend or you used to be, even if they care about me or not; I just want every person I know to know that without them this journey I'm on wouldn't be possible.

(I can name every person I know and say why I am thanking them, but that would take ages, and I don't want to spill any tea.)

And finally, if you're reading this, I thank you too.

Lili's Playlist

Hard to Sleep - Gracie Abrams

Iris - The Goo Goo Dolls

Look Up At The Stars - Shawn Mendes

A Million Dreams - P!nk

willow - lonely witch version - Taylor Swift

birthday cake - Dylan Conrique

In My Blood - Shawn Mendes

Falling - Harry Styles

I Don't Wanna Live Forever - ZAYN, Taylor Swift

Dream - Shawn Mendes

Enchanted (Taylor's Version) - Taylor Swift

broken - lovelytheband

Afterglow - Taylor Swift

I Think I'm In Love - Kat Dahlia

seven - Taylor Swift

marjorie - Taylor Swift

Thightrope - Michelle Williams

Snow On The Beach (feat. More Lana Del Rey) - Taylor Swift, Lana Del Rey

Wonder - Shawn Mendes

Visiting Hours - Ed Sheeran

Delicate - Taylor Swift

The Archer - Taylor Swift

Family Line - Conan Gray

The blue - Gracie Abrams

www.ingramcontent.com/pod-product-compliance
Lightning Source LLC
LaVergne TN
LVHW051053180726
843512LV00019B/1450